Arctic Connection

by

Carol Henry

Connection Series

Arctic Connection

Cover Art by *The Wild Rose Press, Inc.*

The Wild Rose Press, Inc.
PO Box 708
Adams Basin, NY 14410-0708
Visit us at www.thewildrosepress.com

Publishing History
First Edition, 2024
Trade Paperback ISBN 978-1-5092-5343-2
Digital ISBN 978-1-5092-5344-9

Connection Series
Published in the United States of America

Dedication

To my very own High School Sweetheart, my hero, best friend, and travel buddy—my husband, Gary. Once again a tribute to our own great Arctic adventure up along the Norwegian coast and the North Cape—the top of the world.

Acknowledgments

A very special thanks to Ingrid Lunde for her insights into her Norwegian fishing family's operation, her reading of my initial draft, and her friendship. To my various writing partners, and to my sister for slogging through my final rough draft, I send a gratitude of thanks. And to my editor, Josette and her wonderful magic wand.

Reluctantly, Brianna followed Conner back to their vehicle. The weather was ideal, and she was loath to leave this spectacular setting behind. But this wasn't a vacation, and there were many more scenic sites to enjoy along the way. Still, they had work to do. She climbed into the car, buckled her seat belt, and sighed. She was glad she'd agreed to join him on this impromptu expedition. She couldn't wait to share her memories with her parents when she returned stateside.

Conner leaned out the window to double-check for oncoming traffic before pulling out of the parking area. Finding it clear, he slowly maneuvered the SUV onto the highway. A large, tan-colored van came careening recklessly over the knoll, heading right at them on the wrong side of the road. Conner veered to the right in order to avoid a head-on collision. The oncoming vehicle, instead of correcting its path, swerved directly toward them, their front bumper hitting against the SUV's right back fender. The loud crash twisted their SUV sideways, causing its rear end to bang back against the guardrails, next to the overhang, heading in the opposite direction.

Brianna was thrown against the inside of the door, hitting her shoulder. She screamed, then held her breath, closed her eyes, and hoped the railing was sturdy enough to keep them from careening over the cliff and the mile-high drop-off into the rocky ledge and gushing water far below.

Praise

ARCTIC CONNECTION:
"There may be something fishy going in the Arctic waters, but it's Brianna Murphy and Conner Holt who are quickly hooked—on each other. As their investigation heats up, so does their romantic connection, in Carol Henry's latest action-packed novel of romantic suspense."

~Therese Walsh, author

SHANGHAI CONNECTION:
"Carol Henry's beautifully written descriptions immerse you in the surroundings…edge-of-the-seat thrills…"

~Mal Olson, author

Other books in Carol Henry's Connection Series:
Amazon Connection
Shanghai Connection
Rio Connection
Cairo Connection

Prologue

Sven Olson couldn't believe his bad luck. What in the hell was Brianna Murphy doing in Bergen? Spotting her coming off the Fløibanen Funicular while he stood in line behind the bustling crowd waiting to board, he quickly ducked behind a stocky man with a tall cap on his large head, his hair springing out over his ears. He hoped she hadn't seen him watching her. It had to be her. Despite her Norwegian background, her strawberry blonde hair stuck out like a sore thumb. He'd heard enough about her to be wary of her presence in Norway, especially as she was part of the federation's team to inspect the coastal waters here in Norway.

Spotting Brianna Murphy didn't bode well. How much did she know about him? Had she found out about his connection to Maine through the Wild and Wonderful Organization, and now Norway's decline in fish? Had they put her on his trail?

Dammit! He was on his way to meet with his Italian contacts at the café at the top of the Fløien mountainside. He had to keep her in his sights to make sure he stayed out of hers. He wasn't sure she would recognize him. He was going to have to be vigilant and find out what she was up to and what she knew. And it didn't help that Bob Wilkins had also been appointed on the federation's team. What was the federation thinking?

What the hell were they doing here in Norway?

1

He waited until the passengers finally disembarked the funicular. When the coast was clear, he joined the others, making a mad dash to get on board seconds before the doors shut. He slid into the first vacant seat available, thankfully far away from Ms. Murphy, as the cog-train-type vehicle shifted into gear and started its incline up the mountainside. He kept his head averted, staring out the window, unaware of the scenery whizzing by outside.

He'd recently volunteered to assist the Norwegian Fishing Federation with their Arctic Project. The team was assigned the task of investigating the decline in fish along the coast and especially the Barents Sea. Assisting the committee would enable him to play it straight and keep the authorities off their tails.

A lot of money was riding on it. He had to warn Gianni before all hell broke loose.

Chapter One

Brianna leaned against the railing and gazed out over Bergen from atop Fløien Mountain, one of the Seven Mountains making up the magnificent area surrounding Bergen and the North Atlantic. The bright afternoon sun sparkled off the Vågen waters in the Bryggen Harbor area, the Gulf Stream in the distance— the gateway to the fjords. A keen sense of homecoming washed over her. It'd been several years since she'd visited her mother's family in Norway—her family. However, this visit was overshadowed by the purpose of her research assignment.

She let out a deep sigh, zipped up her lightweight blue jacket to ward off the cool breeze, and tucked wisping strands of strawberry blonde hair behind her ears. She gazed out over the bustling community far below. Fisherman's Wharf teemed with activity. Unfortunately, her uncle's fishing operation up along the coast in Tromsø was one of several sites the joint teams were instructed to investigate. Bob Wilkins, her cohort from Wild and Wonderful, had indicated there was more amiss than the federation was willing to admit. As far as he was concerned, the decline in fish in the coastal waters off Norway, especially up along the Arctic and Barents Seas, had little to do with natural causes or climate change. He hadn't been specific. But he had mentioned a local from Lobster Cove, Sven Olson, who had followed his family when they moved back to Bergen to run their family's fish farm.

Was there a connection here somewhere? Or was Bob grasping at straws, trying to prove to Wild and Wonderful that he was worthy of his investigative position with the company? From the short time she'd spent with Bob Wilkins, she found him to be negative, a bit outspoken, and adamant that the loss of "catch" in Norway had nothing to do with climate change. Her boss, Helen Mapes, owner of Wild and Wonderful, hadn't commented on Bob's theories one way or the other.

It was going to be an interesting assignment.

She pulled her jacket collar around her neck and wrapped her cozy neck scarf more snugly to ward off the brisk May wind whipping over the Seven Mountains' viewing area. She caught her long ponytail, adjusted her headband, and then made her way through the throng of tourists toward the café at the top of the hill. She could use a cup of coffee to help dispel the chill that was beginning to set in while standing out in the cold breeze. Instead of finding a place to sit inside the café, she decided to order a coffee and catch the funicular back down to the busy harbor far below. The café was packed already with a short order line. Waiting her turn, she scanned the cozy room, wondering if everyone here was a tourist or a local who simply liked coming to the top of the mountain to enjoy a morning coffee and take in the scenic splendor, as she did.

Finally, a mocha latte in hand, she ambled back to the station where she waited for the funicular to wind its way up the hillside to carry the passengers back down. Once on board, she settled in an empty seat at the rear of the vehicle next to a window on the left where she had an optimal, unobstructed view of the town, harbor, and fjords.

Brianna sipped her coffee and concentrated on meeting with the Norwegian Fishing Federation's Arctic Project members later that afternoon. Who were they? How many had been chosen to participate in this project? She hadn't met them yet but knew it was comprised of her and Bob Wilkins from Wild and Wonderful, a climatologist from Seattle, and several members from Norway and Russia. She'd meet them all this afternoon, but right now she needed this time alone to prepare her inner psyche in order to deal with the possibility of her uncle's involvement. Not wanting to go behind her family's backs, she knew she was going to do just that. She was going to have to keep her own counsel until there was definite proof that they were either part of the suspected ring of profiteers reporting the overall decline in fish catch, or not.

Hopefully, her uncle's fishing operation in Tromsø wasn't involved, and they had a bona fide explanation for their lower-than-usual catch. Granted, she wasn't there to investigate wrongdoing, but her research as a marine biologist would add to the federation's decision-making on global warming practices at the end of the two-week assignment.

The ride down the mountainside took minutes, enough time for Brianna to adjust to being in Norway again, switch focus, and try to enjoy the view as the funicular clacked down the tracks. With additional time on her hands before she met with the Norwegian Fishing Federation to go over the Arctic Project Teams' assignments, she stepped off the funicular when it reached the bottom of the hillside, turned left onto Torget Street, and headed for the outdoor fish market.

The large market hugging the harbor teemed with the overwhelming fragrance of fresh-caught seafood, the sea, and an underlying scent of diesel from the marina. The huge roadside-type market offered everything imaginable, including homegrown vegetables brought to market and tantalizing baked goods. Several mini outdoor restaurants offered dining on an assortment of delicacies while diners overlooked the bustling harbor and watched the ships come and go. The area was already packed with locals and tourists alike.

Drawn to an Asian vendor serving a seafood and rice broil, she couldn't resist the aroma of fresh herbs and spices steaming in a caldron-size wok or the sight of the tantalizing, colorful dish that had steam rising around the Asian-looking cook. The woman stood under a large tented area, her dark hair pulled back, accentuating her dark smiling eyes as she stirred the concoction with a giant-size ladle. She wore a chef's white apron that covered her long slender body and a bright-red silk blouse and dark trousers underneath.

Brianna quickly dug in her shoulder purse for a few kroner and handed them over in exchange for a large portion of the curried seafood over white rice. Scanning the crowded area where others were enjoying the day's delicacies in search of a place to sit, she spotted several picnic tables near the edge of the dock with empty seats. She made her way over to one of the empty tables and sat down. The wind wasn't as strong in the protected harbor as it had been on top of the mountain, as a couple of cruise ships were blocking the air flow. She gladly unzipped her jacket, set it on the bench next to her, and proceeded to dig in to her savory meal. The warm spices melded together in a combination that was both satisfying and filling.

A few minutes later, she was surprised to find her boss approach.

"May I join you?" Helen Mapes, owner of Wild and Wonderful Corporation and the epitome of efficiency, stood next to her table, lunch in hand. An older woman, she was dressed conservatively, with a navy-blue suit jacket over a white blouse, her hair pulled back in a French twist.

"Of course, Helen. I was going to look you up when I returned to the hotel before the meeting to make sure we were on the same page."

"Yes, well, we do have a few things to discuss before the meeting this afternoon. But I won't be sailing on the same boat with you." Helen chuckled. She placed her takeout on the table and slid onto the bench opposite Brianna.

"I was pleased you took the time from your business in France to come to Norway." Brianna took a sip from her soft drink, giving Helen a chance to settle in. "With you sitting in on the meeting, it will give us a heads-up, credential-wise, with the federation." She knew Helen, and the Wild and Wonderful Corporation, were highly regarded around the world, having completed major projects as far as South America, Egypt, and China. Having the owner of the company show up in person was always an honor.

But why did Helen want to talk to her prior to the meeting with the Arctic Project Team without Bob Wilkins present? Bob, also employed by Wild and Wonderful, had arrived in Bergen yesterday, but Brianna hadn't met with him yet.

Helen took a moment to indulge in her lobster roll and sip from her coffee. "I wish I could stay longer. I just love Norway this time of year. One of these days I'm going to take a leisurely sail up the coast on one of these voyages instead of rushing from spot to spot. The scenery alone is worth the expense, but I'd like to take the time to enjoy it and the touristy trap sites. I'm a bit jealous you'll get to see it at a semi-leisurely pace. But, as they say, 'duty calls.' I'm still working in several wine country vineyards in France, so I need to get back. In the meantime, I felt it was more important for me to fly to Bergen to set the tone for our involvement here in Norway. I don't want any misconceptions about what Wild and Wonderful is all about. Bob can be outspoken and forward. He's a decent man, don't get me wrong, but I know him. He can have a bee in his bonnet and not let it go."

"You sound concerned. Is there something specific I need to be aware of?"

"First, I want to say how sorry I am about your parents' ill health and that I wasn't in the country at the time to be there for you."

Brianna was still concerned for their health. She hoped she could fully concentrate on the assignment at hand once the program got underway. She needed to concentrate on her uncle's situation. Was he even one of those under scrutiny by the federation?

"Thank you, Helen. I understand your constraints. I hope things are going well for you in France."

"A few drawbacks, but doable. But as you surmise, I think there might be a problem here, thus, why I included Bob Wilkins in on the research team." Helen sighed, her tone resigned. She looked out over the harbor, down at her food, then directly into Brianna's eyes. In a lowered voice she said, "I want you to be very vigilant. I don't mean to scare you, but there have been a few serious accidents with several of the previous team members while investigating the situation here in Norway. That's why the federation has stepped up. I know there is much to be said for global warming, but word has it that there might be something more going on besides aquifer pollution or climate change that is decimating the fish population."

"How so?" Brianna's appetite dwindled despite the enticing meal in front of her. She crossed her arms along the edge of the table and waited for Helen to elaborate.

"One of the reasons Wild and Wonderful was asked to participate in this operation is the fact that Bob Wilkins was inadvertently connected to an investigation back in Maine a couple of years ago, before he joined our team."

"Bob did mention the incident in passing. Something about a black-market ring, but he didn't elaborate. How does that impact our research here in Norway?" Brianna watched as Helen dug into her lobster roll. Taking advantage of her boss enjoying her meal, she spooned a good portion of her own shrimp and rice into her mouth, the curry seasoning warming her insides.

"They think there is still a tie between the black market there and here in Norway," Helen commented. "They think there is a 'mole' of sorts working within the program. You need to be alert, just in case. I wanted to warn you while I had the chance. Be careful. I want you to report anything unusual to your team advisor. Immediately."

Was this what Bob had been referring to? Was there a connection between Lobster Cove and the situation here in Norway? Was there a connection between that ring and her uncle's operation?

The teams hadn't been assigned yet. Brianna knew that would happen at this afternoon's meeting. But she was suddenly concerned about her involvement in the entire operation. Was she in danger? Or were Helen's concerns a result of Bob's theory? She pushed her dish aside and looked up at her boss.

"Helen, you're scaring me. What am I supposed to be looking for? How is this connected to the Maine operation that Bob was involved in?"

"Talk to Bob. He'll fill you in if he hasn't already. As you know, the main point of our research is to discover the real cause of the decline of fish here in the Arctic region. The 'set' catch from the various countries and in this region is one thing; the amount that they are actually hauling in has drastically declined."

Brianna knew the particulars. Hopefully, working with the entire team would be safety in numbers. "What about you, Helen? How long will you be here in Norway?"

"Just for the day. As I said, I need to get back to France. I'll attend the joint meeting to make sure everything is on track. I'm going to do a quick jaunt up along the coast to check in on a few of our sites. I'll fly back to France day after tomorrow. In the meantime, you have my cell phone number if you need anything major. I'm out in the vineyards a lot. If you can't reach me, give Darla a call back at headquarters in New York. She'll relay any urgent messages, and I'll get back to you as soon as I can."

Darla Slidell, a disgruntled researcher at Wild and Wonderful, who had been passed over in regard to several international assignments, was actually a very informed and pleasant woman. Brianna had had no trouble working with her, and they had even formed a solid friendship. Despite her cluttered and seemingly disorganized office, Darla was on top of things and kept Wild and Wonderful running smoothly when Helen was engaged in projects out of the country.

Helen finished her lobster roll in silence, drained her coffee, and stood. "I'll see you at the meeting this afternoon at two. Enjoy your lunch."

Brianna watched her boss gather her empty meal wrapping, stand, toss the trash in a nearby receptacle, and disappear through the crowded fish market. Now what? Helen Mapes was known by her employees to be an elusive but effective CEO. She gave her employees the authority to do their job without her interference. She trusted them, even though her assignments were sometimes not always clear-cut. Like now. What the heck was she supposed to be on the lookout for? And who? And did Bob Wilkins know more than he was letting on?

Wild and Wonderful Corporation was a well-respected grassroots organization that had gained a stellar reputation for helping to obtain contracts internationally. Whether to improve their economy, make sure other companies or institutions weren't overstepping environmental standards, as well as endangering people, flora, and fauna in the wild, Helen Mapes had built the business into a much sought-after enterprise in New York's Finger Lakes Region. Brianna was lucky to be chosen to replace Megan Holloway, who had met and married Helen's cousin, Jordan Kaine, and moved to Florida to continue working from there. Although Brianna had only been with the company a year, it had been an eye-opener, a learning experience, and a comfortable fit. Being asked to work on this assignment in Norway as a marine biologist was icing on the cake. Maybe.

Only time would tell.

Brianna finished her meal and wandered back to her hotel along the Bryggen district's main street. The air was brisk but pleasant. The sidewalk was packed with locals and visitors alike as they shopped in the various novelty shops along the way. Many, like her, strolled along the walkway, window shopping. Spotting several statues of trolls in one of the windows, she was reminded of Darla's parting shot as she had left the office to catch her flight to Norway.

"Watch out for all those trolls, Brie. They aren't the little darlings they're purported to be. They can be mean little buggers. Cute, but not to be trusted."

She'd tried to reassure Darla that she was part Norwegian and paid no-never-mind to those silly legends. Perhaps she'd buy one for Darla before she left Norway. The uglier, the better.

The hotel she was assigned in Bergen was located farther down the street behind the colorful row of 200-year-old wooden houses from the Hanseatic era. She entered the hotel's revolving doors and crossed past the reception desk toward the elevators. The modern interior was spacious, with several easy chairs and short sofas arranged conversational-style with small tables snuggled next to them. The elegant décor sported crystal chandeliers overhead and overstated seasonal flower centerpieces on the circular glass-topped tables scattered around the room. Guests were in various stages of coming and going, pulling luggage behind them.

She checked her watch as she approached the elevator. She had just enough time to go to her room, freshen up, and meet with the committee. She wanted to make a good first impression. She was a bit nervous but eager to meet everyone and get to know them before heading out on assignment. According to Helen, they were a multicultural group and were touted to be the best in their fields. She hoped she measured up to their standards.

The elevator doors swished open. She pushed the button for the fourth floor, and the door closed. Alone in the enclosure, she let out a deep breath and vowed she was going to keep a professional persona. Keep her eyes and ears open for whatever Helen thought was out there, and help prove that her family wasn't involved in anything shady.

****

Sven Olson waited until he was sure Ms. Murphy was out of sight and then stepped off the funicular. He kept his head down as he headed for the café on the side of the hill, entered, and found an empty table way in the back of the crowded room. He claimed it quickly, scanned the room to make sure Ms. Murphy wasn't there, and then ordered a beer and waited for his contact to arrive. Although their latest shipment was targeted for the Asian markets, it was scheduled to funnel through Italy first. Thus, his major contact Gianni Santino. He hadn't anticipated the federation to develop such a large expedition to address the concern of the loss of fish in the Norwegian coastal waters, as well as the lost income to the fishing businesses in the area. He had been assured that Gianni's men had not overfished and instead had taken small quantities from various locations up along the coast so as not to warrant attention. The damn fools hadn't listened. Now they had to be more careful.

Sven looked up over his beer to find Gianni breezing through the bar's door as if it were just another day of grabbing a cup of cheer. If it weren't for him being in charge of the operation, he'd be a bit concerned at Gianni's heavyset, dark, brooding persona. He was followed by his two lackeys. The taller man was definitely Asian—dark-olive skin, jet-black hair, and eyes that glared at him. The shorter of the two, by a head, was harder to define. But it didn't matter in the least. They'd better be good at their jobs. Everyone stood to make a bundle on their latest haul they had prearranged. Having the federation stick their nose in now could prove detrimental. Sven hoped he could divert the federation's teams' attention away from Gianni and their operation. Seeing as he was on the federation's payroll and part of the investigating team, he was hoping he could divert everyone's attention.

"Good afternoon, gentlemen. Have a seat." Sven stood as the men approached. He indicated the wooden chairs next to the square table.

All three men dragged the heavy chairs out from under the table and plunked down without ceremony. The men had no sooner removed their hats than a young, blushing, full-bodied, blonde waitress arrived, took their order, and left. Sven didn't blame her for rushing off. These men looked as menacing as they obviously were.

"I hope you don't mind if I make this short," Sven addressed the men, eyeing each in turn. He didn't trust them, but it was the price one paid when one was involved in this type of operation. "I have an important gathering with the federation in a half hour, and I don't want to miss it. If I don't show up, it might look suspicious. And we all know we don't need that."

"What? You are meeting with their teams?" Gianni demanded. "Will this not draw more attention to you? Our operation?"

The man's expression was disconcerting. Was the Italian questioning his loyalty to them? His primary status in their operation?

"The opposite." Sven took a draw on his beer before answering. "It will allow me to be able to monitor the situation, as I have been selected to serve on one of the teams. With my fishing background and connection to the federation in that capacity, I can quickly deflect any inkling that I am involved. If they get too close to us, I can head them off in another direction if need be. They have enlisted a climatologist to prove that it is nothing more than global warming, climate change, that is causing the decline in fish. We can use his influence to deflect the federation from our activities. If all goes well, you can get in and out without detection. But it is best you take precaution and do not linger in any one location too long. I will make a copy of the federation's schedule of intended stops up along the coast as soon as I get a copy this afternoon. I'll leave it in our usual drop-off location. Try to stay one step ahead or, if necessary, a step behind. In fact, if you stay a step behind, then their catch statistics won't reflect our take."

"Excellent," Gianni exclaimed. He picked up his mug of beer and toasted the others. "We have our boat in the harbor ready to head up the coast. Where is our final pickup location this time? Will you be there or someone else?"

"I have made arrangements at two locations along the Norwegian Sea. Small fishing villages. You will stop at three locations along the way, but the bigger haul will be in Tromsø and farther up along the cape. You should be aware of a Mr. Bjorn Kelsey in Tromsø or the captain of his fishing fleet. He is one of the major fishing farms in the area. If you come in contact with him, he must think you are legit, so you must fly the Norwegian flags. And make sure one of our local fishermen is with you for verification. Here are the papers to give him if need be."

Sven handed over several legal-looking documents. "If you run into any unforeseen trouble, contact me immediately. Do not give them my name. Otherwise, I won't be able to defuse the situation."

"Do not cross us," Gianni grumbled, his gaze darting to the two heavyset men on either side of him who had remained quiet the entire time before turning his dark glare at Sven.

"I have no intention of doing so," Sven assured the Italian. "Why would I? I have as much to lose as you."

Gianni's two cronies didn't say a word but nodded in agreement, as if they understood English and had followed the entire conversation.

"I will be in Tromsø a week from today," Sven said. "Meet me at our usual location and make sure you have the amount we discussed. Now, if you gentlemen will excuse me, I have a meeting to get to before they miss me."

Sven rose, threw a handful of change on the table for his beer, and stepped around the blonde waitress who had just come to deliver his cronies' orders. He crossed his fingers as he left to take the funicular back down off the mountain. He hadn't seen Gianni's two cohorts before, and they certainly didn't look as if he could trust either of them. *Shit*. He was going to have to do something more than cross his fingers. He was going to have to keep on his toes.

So much for being worried about the Russian delegation who were investigating their own situation. It was a good thing he didn't have ports to check out on their side of the Barents Sea. He'd convinced Gianni to steer clear of that location. Otherwise, the whole operation could turn into an international incident. He was beginning to think he should have stayed back in Lobster Cove and taken over his parents' flower shop before they sold it.

Chapter Two

Brianna sat at the elongated wooden table in the hotel's conference center along with Bob Wilkins and Helen Mapes. To her right, Maxwell Erickson, CEO of the Norwegian Fishing Federation and director of the Arctic Project, fussed with papers in front of him while he waited for everyone to be seated.

Scattered around the table, to her left, were the federation's board of directors and members from the Norwegian scientific community. But her attention was drawn to the man who had just entered the room—Conner Holt, the scientist from Seattle who specialized in climate change. She recognized his face as soon as he'd come through the glass-plated double doors across the room, thanks to his picture in the scientific journal she'd read on the flight across the Atlantic. But she hadn't been prepared for the man now seated across from her. The late afternoon sun shone through the panel of curtainless windows behind her and illuminated him like a beacon. Not only was he much more handsome in person, but he wasn't the behind-the-desk researcher or pale scientist poring over data, trends, and weather patterns his picture had depicted him to be. The well-attired man who had been outfitted in a stark-white formal shirt, navy suit, and red tie with his dark hair groomed to perfection was nowhere in sight. Her breath caught as he sat down opposite her. Casually dressed,

Conner Holt resembled a rodeo bronco rider. He might not have the appropriate attire, but he sure looked like he knew his way around a corral. With his wind-blown dark hair, tanned skin tones, and solid body, not to mention his self-assured gait and a smile that made her wonder what he was thinking, he scanned the occupants in the room. She had pegged him all wrong.

"So, ladies and gentlemen," Mr. Erickson began, tapping his pencil on the notepad in front of him to gain everyone's attention. "You all know why we are here. However, there are a few people I'd like you to meet and get acquainted with before you get underway with your assignments." Pointing his pencil in Helen's direction, he introduced her. "Although Ms. Mapes won't be with us on this journey, her specialists in the field of marine biology, Ms. Brianna Murphy and Mr. Robert Wilkins, are on board to help with the investigation on her behalf." He indicated each of them in turn with his pencil.

The others nodded greetings in their direction.

"Thank you, Mr. Erickson." Helen leaned forward and addressed everyone present. "We're pleased to have been invited to help with the investigation of the decline of fish, specifically cod, here in Norway. I can assure you that Ms. Murphy and Mr. Wilkins are both highly qualified to be included in this important project. You won't be disappointed, I'm sure."

"That's good to know," Mr. Erickson said, then perused those around the table. "There has been a lot of bio prospecting in the area. We want to make sure it isn't harming the aquifer and marine life. Therefore, we have invited Mr. Conner Holt to assist with the possibility of the effects of climate change in the area." He nodded at

Mr. Holt. Everyone turned their heads in his direction as Mr. Erickson continued. "Along with the other local qualified members gathered here today, I have assigned everyone into two separate groups. This will add a higher degree of insight into the investigation. So at the end of your research, we will meet again to compare your assessments, and the federation will take it from there."

Brianna had a hard time paying attention once she'd glanced across the table at Conner Holt and caught him smiling at her. What seemed like minutes were only seconds before Conner Holt's lips tilted upward in a side grin, and he gave a brief but telling nod in her direction, indicating he'd caught her staring at him, before he turned his attention back to Mr. Erickson. Her insides heated, and she was sure her face had turned red from being caught checking him out. She inwardly shook her head. After her disastrous breakup with Carl six months ago, she wasn't ready to succumb to the male species anytime soon. She focused her attention on Mr. Erickson, hoping she hadn't missed anything important.

"I only have one item on the agenda," the director continued, as he scanned the occupants assembled around the table once more before consulting the paper in front of him. "That is, to assign the various teams. You will be working very closely with each other over the next few weeks. Hopefully, you will be able to help us solve this problem of the declining fish in the surrounding shores and especially the North Cape and the Barents Sea. As you know, many of the fisheries are losing money this past year due to the decline in cod as well as haddock. So, with that in mind, each team will have a meteorologist and a marine biologist on board to include members from our Norwegian and Russian delegations."

Everyone sat quietly, waiting for their respective assignment as Mr. Erickson sipped from his water glass, cleared his throat, and shuffled his papers again.

"Team One's leader is Sondra Sølreida, with Robert Wilkins, Stefan Dutlov, and Sven Olson."

Brianna's head shot up at the mention of Sven Olson's name. *Oh, my God!* Was this the same Sven Olson who Bob had mentioned in connection with the Lobster Cove incident? She'd never met Mr. Olson so didn't recognize the man sitting at the far end of the table. The man was obviously Norwegian, with that full head of sand-white blond hair and deep-blue eyes that seemed to be assessing everyone around the table. She looked over at Bob Wilkins in order to gauge his reaction and wasn't surprised to see the cautious look on his face. She turned to Helen and noticed that she was quietly concentrating on making notes on her tablet.

Chills ran up her spine. What the hell was going on here? Something wasn't right in Denmark. Well, okay, Norway. What had Helen gotten her involved in? She was going to have to have a conversation with her boss before Helen returned to France.

Mr. Erickson continued, "Team Two's leader is Lars Jensen, with Conner Holt, Brianna Murphy, and Ivan Alexander."

OMG! Conner Holt was part of her team. Her face warmed again. *Damn.* She was going to have to keep her mind focused on the project, not the handsome man sitting across from her. She grasped the folder in front of her, hoping Mr. Holt hadn't witnessed her reaction.

Mr. Erickson proceeded to outline the agenda. "As this is a fact-finding mission only, whether it is climate change or something amiss with the aquifer, you will report to your team leader, who will then report to me. I've arranged transport up along the coast to Tromsø, then on to Honningsvåg, the North Cape, and the Barents Sea. There are several fishing operations you'll need to visit in between. Those operations in particular have seen a drastic decline in recent months. There is a list of these specific locations, as well as others along the route, in your folders in front of you. If you have any questions, your team leader can help. You will take the ship up the coast to Ålesund. Rental vehicles and equipment will be on board the steamer for your use. Departure time is eight o'clock tomorrow morning, sharp. In the meantime, my assistant, Johanna, has arranged a 'meet and greet' at Harry's Bar just down the street along the pier. I'll meet you there at six this evening."

Brianna had quickly skimmed the list of fisheries being affected, and was aware her family's operation was included. Did Helen know Bjorn Kelsey was her uncle? And if she did, again, was that why she had been chosen for this particular assignment? And how was Sven Olson really involved? Was Bob holding back? Did he know more than he was letting on? Did climate change really have anything to do with the problem here in Norway? It didn't matter. Helping to prove that her family's operation wasn't involved in anything nefarious was going to be her main goal. She would be ever more vigilant checking out the marine life and habitat.

****

Brianna entered Harry's Bar and Grill, along with Bob Wilkins, and was immediately struck by the interior's fishing décor that surrounded her. Seasoned pine boards lining the walls were covered with historic fishing paraphernalia. She couldn't mistake the fact that this was an establishment catering to fishermen. The bar, tables, chairs, and even the flooring spoke of marine life. Illusions of foaming waves washing along the sideboards were sketched in an aqua and frothing white. A border circling the edge of the ceiling highlighted various fish in their authentic colors.

Looking at those already assembled in the adjacent room as they made their way toward the other members of both teams now gathered at the far end of the bar, Bob snarked. "I guess this is where you and I get to discover what everyone else is really thinking in regard to this 'fact-finding' mission."

"What do you mean?" She stopped, reached out, and stayed him with her hand on his arm, not wanting to have this conversation surrounded by the others. "What are you intimating, Bob? I have a feeling you think there is more to this fact-finding mission than meets the eye. I saw the surprise on your face when they introduced the members of the panel. One in particular. Sven Olson. What is really going on?" She scanned the room, waiting for Bob's reply. Everyone appeared to be accounted for except Conner Holt. And Sven Olson. "With the assortment of scientists on the panel and the various countries involved, what do you think isn't being said?"

"Is Holt the only climatologist on the committee?" Bob smirked, scanning the room ahead, his eyebrows raised.

"As far as I know, and that should say something about his qualifications."

"This whole expedition is a waste of his time. I really don't think they're looking at climate change to be the cause of the decline in catch. In fact, as I may have mentioned earlier, there was a big black-market ring in Lobster Cove, Maine, a year ago. Seems they were selling to an Asian market that worked through Scandinavia. I find it very odd that Sven Olson worked for his parents' flower shop back in Lobster Cove, then without any notice the entire family up and moved back to Norway. And it wasn't to open a flower shop. It was to take over their family's business here in Bergen. Sven joined them and has been working for them ever since. As a member of the fishing federation here in Norway, he has contacts with many of the outfits along the coast. And he left Lobster Cove a week before all hell broke loose there. Think about it."

"Like you said, he wasn't involved with the fishing industry while he was in Lobster Cove and wasn't in the area when the bust went down. So why are you suggesting he might be up to something here? He's on your team, isn't he?"

"Yes. But although there is no clear-cut indication that he has connections to the black market back in Maine, the coincidence of his leaving just before the case broke and then to be involved in fishing in Norway is a bit 'fishy' if you ask me. Pardon the pun."

She knew Bob didn't think for a single moment that climate warming was the cause of the decline in fish. He had been involved with the investigation in Maine where they discovered the band of fishermen stealing from other fishermen and selling stock on the side to make a profit. Bob had indicated that during their investigation they also discovered that these fishermen had ties to Norway. Thus, Bob's inclination to prove that the decline in fish had nothing to do with global warming. She, on the other hand, hadn't formed an opinion one way or the other. As Helen Mapes and Mr. Erickson had decreed, this was a fact-finding mission. She needed to keep an open mind. But did Helen's assignment of Bob Wilkins to their team have anything to do with her warning to be vigilant? Did Helen know what was really going on? Or at least suspect as much? Again. Did either of them know something relevant that they weren't sharing? And why?

"But why would he undercut his own family's catch?" She scanned the area around them, hoping no one was within hearing distance. "Sven is a member of the federation, as you say."

"I could be jumping to conclusions," Bob said. "But I think we should be vigilant."

As Helen had already stated. Still, Brianna didn't think the authorities would have hired Sven to help solve their dilemma if he hadn't already been vetted. Were both Bob and Helen grasping at straws?

They entered through the open double doors of the bar where several of those in attendance were already holding drinks and nibbling on hors d'oeuvres. Ivan Alexander, a handsome young Russian on their team, was the first to greet them.

"It is my pleasure to formally meet you." His smile was genuine, his bubbly personality contagious. Although his greeting was meant for the both of them, his animated smile and sparkling hazel eyes lingered on her. He was a good-looking man, but she was immune to such charms. Not going there. This was all about work. She was about to return his greeting when Bob stepped up to shake Ivan's hand. Only then did the young man turn from her to accept Bob's hand and acknowledge his presence.

"I understand we have a bit of a problem in regard to the fishing quotas not being recorded properly." Bob's no-nonsense tone was gratingly accusing, even to her ears. "I hope our teams, as well as our countries, can be impartial and open-minded when we discover just what is going on."

Oh, my God! Did Bob just provoke the Russian on day one? Thankfully, Bob was on Team One with Sven Olson and wouldn't be provoking Ivan on a daily basis. They had been briefed on the situation on the joint Norwegian-Russian Commission that was formed in 1976. With the decrease in cod, haddock, and capelin, many suspected that the fish quotas weren't being reported accurately. She was willing to wait until after they had finished assessing the situation before she determined if there were problems with the system and/or the effects of fishing on the Barents Sea ecosystem. Or if in fact climate change played a role in the situation. Bob, however, seemed to be stuck on the idea that there was a black-market connection. Irritating the Russian to try and get information wasn't the way to go about obtaining anything credible.

The young Russian pursed his lips, raised his eyebrows, and practically scowled at Bob. This didn't bode well.

"I'm sure we'll work together to solve the problem one way or the other regardless of whose team we're on, Mr. Alexander," Brianna said in an effort to ease the tension between the two men. She hoped her smile and sincere manner took the bite off of Bob's accusing tone.

"Please, call me Ivan. As you say, we will be working together." Ivan's facial expressions magically improved when he turned to respond to her. His smile didn't diminish as he turned back to Bob. "I understand you will be working on Team One with Stefan. I think the two of you will have much in common. But come. Meet the others. I see your climatologist has just arrived. It will be interesting to see what will be his assessment."

Brianna wanted to shake Bob for his behavior, but instead, she pulled herself together and followed Ivan and Bob across the room to meet the others who were in the process of welcoming Conner Holt. The man's all-imposing self-assurance had heads turning in his direction.

"Speak of the devil," Bob whispered, returning Conner's smile as he sauntered forward and extended his hand in greeting.

Conner reciprocated Bob's greeting, shook Ivan's hand, and then turned to her. Very businesslike, he also extended his hand. His grip was firm, warm, and sent a zing up her arm the minute her fingers were enfolded in his palm. Before they could engage in conversation, the sexy Norwegian Team One leader, Sondra Sølreida, rushed in between her and Bob and practically collided into Conner. The blonde bombshell, tall and dressed outlandishly sexy, was way too obvious. For someone who was the leader of a team, she didn't exude a professional persona. Obviously, she had the credentials; otherwise, the federation wouldn't have chosen her to take part in the project or be the lead.

"Is so nice to meet you, Conner," Sondra cooed, placing her hand on Conner's arm. "Too bad we aren't on the same team. But we will have plenty of opportunity to get to know each other on this excursion. We have many similar stops along the route we will travel."

Conner wondered what he had done to warrant such

a friendly greeting. From the welcoming sexy smile on Sondra's lovely face, he could only thank heaven above that she wasn't on his team. He wouldn't be in close proximity to her on a daily basis. He could tell already that he needed to keep his distance from her obvious interest in him. He didn't need, or want, to get involved with the opposite sex on this assignment. He'd learned his lesson. Those relationships never ended well.

He pasted a smile on his face and stepped back while removing her clinging hand from his arm, and instead offered his hand in greeting. The young woman looked disappointed, as if she had actually expected a hug. Thankfully, Ivan Alexander and Mr. Erickson intervened.

"Mr. Holt," the director of the project said when he drew to a halt beside Conner. "I'm glad to have a few moments with you before you start your inspection of our coastline. Climate warming is touted to be a major cause occurring in much of the world. With the warming of the waters in the Barents Sea, it could be detrimental to our industry. If that is the case, once you and the others have made your determinations, it will be interesting to see what steps we can take to rectify the situation."

"As you know, I've done a bit of research on the topic," Conner replied, eyebrows raised as he panned the faces of those gathered around their conversation. He wished they had dealt with this information at the meeting, but was glad to get it out in the open with the others now. "Until we do a thorough examination of the area, as you suggest, we can only hope the situation is rectifiable. However, it is wise to have included Ms. Murphy and Mr. Wilkins to ensure the aquifer and marine environment isn't causing the problem or at least contributing to it."

"Of course, there could be other problems that you might not be aware of," Bob interjected, having stood by, listening closely to them.

Conner had a feeling he knew where Bob Wilkins was going with his assumptions. He'd heard the rumors and had taken note. And even if they were true, climate change was more than likely the major contributing factor. Time and research would tell.

"I think we can assume that all options are on the table during the investigation," Conner said, as he turned to Brianna Murphy and a couple of the others who had gravitated toward their conversation and were intent on what was being said. Brianna's concentration on their conversation added to her professionalism. "I'm sure Ms. Murphy's expertise, as well as the others, will prove useful."

Was that a gleam of satisfaction in her eyes at his remark? And a hint of a redness in her cheeks? Again? Hopefully, she wasn't going to come on to him as had Sondra.

"You are right," Mr. Erickson confirmed, bringing Conner back to the conversation. "We will wait until all the data has been collected before the federation makes any assumptions one way or the other. It will be up to the council's board to determine how to proceed. Please, in the meantime, I will excuse myself, as I have other commitments. Help yourself to the buffet and drinks. I look forward to everyone's assessments on your return to Bergen in two weeks' time."

His closing remarks successfully ended the conversation before anyone could take exception.

Conner took advantage of the director's suggestion

to visit the buffet, order a drink from the bar, and find a seat at one of the long tables lined up along the windows overlooking the harbor. Bob Wilkins, Sondra Sølreida, Lars Jensen, and Ivan Alexander joined him. But it was Brianna Murphy who drew his attention. He'd been taken in by her beauty when he met her at the meeting this afternoon and was surprised by his attraction to her. Even now, with her blonde hair pulled back in a ponytail, her pale-blue cardigan that matched her deep-blue eyes, he was finding it hard to concentrate on what Bob Wilkins, who sat across from him, was going on about. His tone of voice, however, brought him out of his contemplations centered around Brianna Murphy.

"So what is it that makes you think this could be all about climate change?" Bob asked, a hint of a smirk on his ruddy face and raised eyebrows.

The guy was as outspoken as a rowdy kid and just as annoying. Conner took a drink of his wine. Dear Lord, another climate change nonbeliever. Go figure.

"Good question." Conner gritted his teeth, took another sip of wine, then drew in a deep sigh and answered. "Our research has already proven that the hydrologic changes caused by global warming have caused a significant reduction in the 'sea ice,' which in turn affects the fish in this area. The Barents Sea in particular."

"So, Mr. Holt..." Brianna began, obviously trying to intervene in order to keep the peace.

But Conner interrupted her. "Conner. Please. I think first-name basis is in order seeing as we'll all be working closely together."

"Conner. Are you suggesting that because of the reduction of sea ice, the fish, especially cod and haddock, are dwindling, which accounts for the lower catch rate?"

He watched her closely. Was she, in fact, curious about global warming, or did she want to defuse Bob Wilkins' offensive approach to the program before it got underway? Her obvious tactic in stepping in to prevent an out-and-out argument that the man certainly seemed to be looking for led him to believe she had experience in this regard.

"It's a strong theory," he cautiously replied. "One that I'm here to help determine." He turned to the others in order to gauge their reaction to the overall discussion. He'd indicated he was still open to any additional research the teams uncovered, but he knew many didn't believe in global warming. Even though he had already done extensive research in the Arctic around Iceland and Alaska, it was a hard sell to those who didn't want to believe. Nevertheless, he couldn't resist sharing the facts that he'd already uncovered. Thankfully, it looked as if Ivan Alexander and Lars Jensen were open to the possibility.

"Conner, I've been reading all about your research on climate warming," Sondra interjected, her chin resting against the back of her hand, her elbow leaning on the table, her smile beguiling to anyone who was open to her charms. "I would love to get your take on the findings in our region." Her dusty-green eyes devoured him.

Good Lord, he had to put a stop to the obvious "come-on" signals she was sending his way. "Of course, I have my research to fall back on." He kept his voice evenly controlled, not wanting to send any reciprocating vibes her way. "But as this is a fact-finding mission, I'll have to take a rain check until we have a chance to study the overall data at the end of our investigation. Like I mentioned, it has already been proven that global warming is responsible for the reduction in 'sea ice' in the region."

"Like you say," Bob interjected, "this is a fact-finding mission. We need to be open to interpreting the facts that we uncover."

Conner suspected Bob wasn't about to be contained in his thoughts against climate change, and felt the need to defuse the situation. "I agree," he said. "We all have our work cut out for us. It will be up to the federation to make the final decisions, as Mr. Erickson stated."

Conner was beginning to wonder if the federation's purpose in inviting him as a lead climatologist was the main focus of his background. Or was it because of his lesser-known specialty? Neither team appeared to be open to the idea of climate change. But now that he was here, he was committed to the project. Seeing how things played out with everyone involved was going to be interesting.

Chapter Three

Thankfully, the buffet was still set up when Sven walked into Harry's Bar and Grill. He ordered a beer from the bar and scanned the room until he found members of both teams gathered at a long table next to the window. He took a steadying breath and relaxed when he noticed Mr. Erickson, director of the project, had already left. Stefan Dutlov and Sondra Sølreida spotted him and simultaneously slid their chairs to the side to make room for him to join them.

"Hope I haven't missed any important discussions." Sven smiled as he approached the table. "Sorry, I got held up in traffic and couldn't find a parking spot." The lie tripped off his lips.

"We were just discussing the travel arrangements and accommodations for the next few weeks," Bob Wilkins spoke up. "We've been assigned two SUVs, one for each team, so we can travel comfortably with all the necessary equipment."

"I'm assuming we'll take the ferry up the coastal Gulf Stream through the fjords toward the North Cape?" Sven knew the schedule forward and backward. He'd been in on the federation's planning stages, hoping to divert target areas his men were trolling.

"That's my understanding, too," Sondra, leader of his team, spoke up. "Although I see we have different drop-off points. Our team gets off in Ålesund. We'll check with a couple of the fisheries there before we drive on up the coast."

"I haven't checked our folder yet." Ivan studied those sitting around the table. "Any idea where our team is headed first?"

"As you know, our teams have different schedules. Our team's first stop is Molde," Lars Jensen, Team Two's leader, said. "We do a quick check there, then head on up the coast to gather information at various stops on our way to Tromsø where we'll meet up with each other. We have reservations at the hotel next to the docks a week from today."

"Yes, ours is similar," Sondra confirmed. "But as you say, we have several different stops along the way before we all meet in Tromsø."

Sven was going to have to warn his cohorts to be careful when they arrived in Tromsø. With everyone congregating there, he didn't want their operations to be detected. If luck was on their side, they would be able to hold off making their connections until after the teams conducted their investigative work in that area.

"If you'll excuse me," Lars said, "I have a couple of friends I've arranged to meet this evening while I'm in Bergen, so I'll say good night. I'll catch up with everyone on the ship tomorrow morning." He pushed back from the table, stood, and waved to everyone, then turned and headed toward the exit.

"As a matter of fact, I have to be going as well." Sven apologized to the group, taking advantage of Lars' departure. "I know I've only just got here, but I need to tie up loose ends at home. I'll see you all in the morning." He followed Lars out the door but noted that the rest of the members stood as if to leave as well. Obviously, his and Lars' leaving was the signal to break up the gathering. Good. He wouldn't have to worry about them discussing additional issues in his absence. He needed time to placate his wife, Marta. She wasn't happy knowing he'd be gone for several weeks. Spending the night with her would hopefully placate her. He also needed to inform his father he'd be away from the family fisheries for the next couple of weeks.

And he needed to make sure Gianni and his men were out of sight.

*****

The following morning Brianna finished an early breakfast, went back to her room, and gathered her belongings. She had another hour before boarding the ship. She decided to get a head start, take a walk along the historic Bryggen district, circle around to the fish market, and see if she could find a coffee.

Dressed in navy-blue slacks and a white, long-sleeved blouse, she was wise enough to slip on a heavyweight sweater, knowing the Norwegian morning air along the coast was cool no matter the time of year. Especially on a sailing ship. This morning there was only a slight breeze, and the sun was on the rise, but it was always smart to be prepared.

The day promised to be glorious, a great way to start their expedition. Hopefully, it was a good omen, and Bob's suspicions would turn out to be unfounded. Still, she had to worry about her uncle's fishing operation. If something was amiss there, she hoped it was due to the aquifer, marine life, and even global warming.

Only time would tell.

She followed the aroma of coffee, purchased a medium latte, pulled her carry-on behind her, and found a bench next to the water's edge. She reclined on the bench, crossed her legs, and took a deep sip of the hot liquid. She had plenty of time before boarding the ship. Inhaling a deep breath of the fresh morning air, she then let it out slowly and steadily. After another satisfying sip of her latte, she began to size up her team members. Lars Jensen, team leader, was a tall, thin Norwegian with blond hair cropped short and a well-trimmed mustache. He seemed rather reserved yet paid rapt attention when the others discussed the mission. Ivan Alexander, on the other hand, was a sexy, brash, young Russian who had no problem speaking up and stepping forward. She definitely knew where she stood with him. And Brianna was on notice not to buy into his attraction to her.

Now, Conner Holt was a different kettle of fish. He was handsome, not in a sexy way, but with a warm, caring, and deeply thoughtful manner. Confident in his beliefs, he didn't expound on his knowledge unless called on to do so. But figuring out what was behind his steady smile when he looked her way wasn't as easy. A smile that drew her to him, and that bit of a dimple on his left cheek when he smiled? *Hmmm*. Conner had been dressed in a pair of casual denim slacks and a teal collared sweatshirt yesterday. She'd been surprised to find he'd worn navy-blue sneakers. She looked down at her own white sneakers. *Hmmm. Sneakers.* They had something in common. Not that she was looking for anything. Really.

Tourist season was in full swing. The dock was busy this morning with tourists milling about, visiting the wharf eateries, and making their way to their destinations for the day. One of these days she was going to join the throng of tourists and simply enjoy herself. She had worked too hard to get where she was today that she hadn't had time to really enjoy life. She thought she'd had something special going when she was in college, but that had ended once she discovered her supposed boyfriend, Carl, had been seeing someone else on the side. So much for a love life. She'd decided to spend the rest of her semesters concentrating on her degree and then finding a job she enjoyed. End of story.

Brianna checked the time on her cell phone and realized it was five minutes to boarding. She swallowed the remainder of her coffee, discarded the cup in the trash, and then, gripping her carry-on, headed toward the ship.

Either the other team members had already boarded, or she was early. They were nowhere in sight. She made her way up the plank leading to the huge whale-like open-mouthed entrance. The large ship was more than a ferry transporting vehicles up along the coast. Besides a freighter delivering goods to the various small communities along the entire Norwegian coastline, it served as a luxury cruise ship with an untold number of tourists. But it also served as a means of transportation for locals without vehicles, needing to do business, shop up along the coast, or visit family. With state rooms, dining halls, conference centers, a coffee shop, viewing areas, and a lounge on board, it was going to be a relaxing start to their journey and their first destination.

A ship's steward waited at the top of the wide opening for passengers to be checked in and directed to their assigned rooms. Brianna showed the steward her boarding pass and state room assignment and was guided to her overnight accommodations where she was given her room's key card. Once inside, she was delighted to see the ample stateroom equipped with her own private bath facilities. She wheeled her carry-on across the room, dropped her shoulder bag onto the queen-size bed sporting a colorful quilted coverlet, and sat down on the edge. She took a moment to contemplate her next move. There was no set schedule this morning. A conference had been set up in one of the meeting rooms for the afternoon, after lunch. With time on her hands, she decided to go up on deck and relax as they set sail for the cape.

She exchanged her sweater for a warmer jacket, grabbed her room's key card, and put the "do not disturb" sign on the outside of the door. Although she would only be onboard overnight, she didn't need room service. This portion of the ship was similar to a regular cruise ship with accommodations numbered on either side of the long hallway. Walking down the narrow corridor toward the elevator, she saw two middle-aged passengers waiting for the door to open. Brianna joined them, smiled, and raised the appropriate number of fingers indicating the floor she wanted.

"We are tourists, also." The heavyset woman smiled as she brushed her long brown hair, streaked with gray, behind her ears. "I'm Marian, and this is my husband, Tom." She pointed to the man at her side.

He tilted his bald head in acknowledgment, his portly stomach overlapping his wide black belt holding up his blue jeans. The elevator doors slid open, and he stepped aside to let both her and his wife enter. Once settled inside, he pushed the button for the lobby, and the doors swished shut.

"Is this your first time to Norway?" the woman asked. Her happy face was contagious.

"No. I have family who live in Tromsø," Brianna said. "I've visited them several times before. What about you?"

"It is our first time, and we are loving it already. It's a breathtakingly beautiful country. We can't wait to see the North Cape. We've heard such wonderful stories from our friends who have already been there. Have you been to the North Cape yet?"

"It's on my bucket list this time." She'd been delighted to discover that the North Cape was one of the areas they were scheduled to investigate. Granted, the visit wasn't due to her whimsy of visiting the site, but she was going to take advantage of the opportunity when they arrived in Honningsvåg.

The elevator stopped, and the doors slid open. Brianna waved to the couple as she exited. "Enjoy your excursions."

She headed to the coffee station she'd spotted in a corner of the open lobby when she had boarded. It was currently teeming with customers in search of their early morning fix. Thankfully, there was a semblance of a line of people waiting to order and not the mad crush in some of the smaller venues back home. The two blonde women behind the tall counter looked frazzled as they attempted to keep up with the early morning rush. Still, they each had a smile on their faces, and their clear, creamy complexions free of makeup were refreshing as they greeted each customer.

She ordered a latte when she finally reached the coffee bar. With tumbler in hand, she went up on deck to take in the view as the ship prepared to depart the busy harbor. The backdrop of Bergen from this perspective, with the Seven Mountains rising behind and surrounding the town in the background, was a delight to the senses—a totally different perspective than from atop Fløien mountainside. This time of year the hillsides were a brilliant green, with the many homes dotting the hillside landscape next to the lakes. The streets surrounding the fish market next to the harbor were still bustling and teeming with life.

She leaned against the railing, sipping her latte, and wondered, not for the first time, if she had made the right decision to accept this particular assignment. She had accepted Helen's request mainly because it would give her a chance to visit her aunt and uncle and her cousin Kristina again. It had been five years since her last visit. Plus, this assignment would give her the opportunity to explore more of Norway. The North Cape had been on her bucket list for some time. She agreed with Marian, the woman in the elevator; she had to visit the North Cape. She'd seen pictures of people standing next to the giant globe overlooking the immense Atlantic Ocean spread out below, a tribute erected to pinpoint Europe's northernmost point in Knivskjellodden. She hadn't considered her bucket list when she accepted this assignment, but she intended to make it a priority to take a side trip to visit the site before returning to the States.

The ship turned into the Gulf Stream where tree-lined mountains surrounded the shores and homes and businesses were tucked in between and up along the hillside. As they continued farther north toward the Arctic Circle, tall jagged mountains loomed in the distance. The sun was high in the cloudless, bright-blue sky now, and a cool breeze had her zipping her jacket. She set her coffee down on the deck, steadied it between her feet, pulled her straight hair into a ponytail, picked her coffee cup up, and relaxed against the railing with a deep sigh. She was looking forward to exploring more of Norway despite her reason for being here.

"Your first trip to Norway?" Conner's sexy voice shook her from her contemplations. She couldn't help noticing how fit he looked this morning, how natural he appeared as he stood next to her, hands in his pants pockets, as if he belonged on the open seas. Like it was an everyday occurrence. She turned from him and gazed back out over the crystal-blue ocean. The color of Conner's eyes.

"Actually, no. My mother's relatives live in Norway. It's been a while since I've visited, but I never tire of the beauty and the soothing ambiance of sailing the fjords up to Tromsø where they live." This was the second time this morning she was asked this question. Did she look like someone who hadn't stepped foot outside the borders of New York State? A novice traveler? She wasn't a world traveler by any means, but she had ventured out and about a couple of times. But the mention of her family back in the States made her heart dip. They would have loved to join her on this trip, especially her mother, if for no other reason than to join in a family reunion at her mother's brother's family home. She had talked to her parents yesterday, and they assured her they were doing well.

"So you've done this often?" Conner asked, leaning against the railing next to her.

"Not often. I've only visited the family a couple of times. The last time was five years ago with my parents."

"Are you planning to visit them while you're here?"

Didn't he know who they were? That they were suspect? That both teams would be accessing her uncle's fishing operation in Tromsø? Or was this his way of digging for information?

"Yes." She sipped from her tumbler, then rested her hands along the railing, mindless of the vibration from the ship's motor as they continued up the coast. "In fact, that's one of our stops. My uncle Bjorn Kelsey owns a fishing operation in Tromsø. It's on our list of sites to investigate. I'm sure you're familiar with the locations we've been assigned to observe." Again, her heart took a dive as she considered the possibility that her uncle might be involved. Or at least the operation as a whole.

"Have they been seeing a decline in their catch as well?" Conner leaned against the railing, clasped his hands together, and looked out to sea, not meeting her eyes.

He stood much too close. She took a deep breath before answering.

"Apparently. Otherwise, we probably wouldn't be visiting his operation. Although I haven't talked to them since I arrived in Norway, they do know we will be visiting. Our team has an appointment with them at the end of the week."

"Do they know you're on the team?"

"Yes. I've contacted them, and they are aware I'm working with the federation. I'm not sure they know they are implicated in wrongdoing. And according to Helen Mapes, they're willing to help in any way they can. Knowing them, I'm sure they will cooperate fully." At least she hoped they would. She had no reason whatsoever to believe that they were hiding something or to doubt that their operation was on the up and up.

"We have a few more ports to inspect before we get there." Conner turned toward her, stepped back, but kept his hand on the railing. "I plan to check out a couple of smaller fishing operations inland before we make our first stop up along the coast. I want to find out if there are any signs of climate changes farther inland that will give me something to compare with our findings along the coastal waters."

Conner was standing much too close. She stepped back, her feet braced slightly apart for leverage, her right hand grasping the ship's railing. She wasn't sure where he was going with this change of topic, but couldn't help asking, "Won't that take away from your research on the ports that are already on our list?"

"I've done some preliminary research on a couple of the smaller locations already and have interviewed a couple of the locals last week. Wanted to get a broader handle on the situation."

"Already?" She faced him with raised eyebrows. "How long have you been in Norway?"

His smile was disarming and hard to resist. She dismissed it, however, and continued to question him with a raised eyebrow.

"A couple of weeks. Seeing as I'm the only climatologist on the panel, I wanted to check out some of the smaller fishing communities to have something to compare with the locations we've been assigned. And a few that Team One is checking out that we aren't."

"And what have you discovered?"

"Nothing new or inconsistent with what's already been determined. I'm planning on taking a side trip when we get to Måløy when we dock. I'm going to head out to Geiranger and the area around Trondheim Fjord to check out the various fishing outlets in that area. It's quite the tourist attraction. Have you ever visited that part of

Norway?"

Again, where was he going with this questioning? Was he curious about her credentials in being chosen for their team? Or was he getting personal? And what did one have to do with the other?

"Mostly our visits were to Bergen and then along the coast to stay with family in Tromsø," she answered truthfully, still wondering where this switch in conversation was leading. Although she had often thought about venturing farther inland when visiting her family in Tromsø, they had always remained close to family. "I haven't visited much of the inland areas, but I have knowledge of my uncle's business."

"Why not join me? It's a perfect opportunity for you to check out the aquifer at a couple of the locations that have also complained of low catch in fish. I've made arrangements to use the SUV that's been provided for our team. It won't be needed until we get to Molde, so Lars has given me the go-ahead. It's a good day's drive, and we can pick up the ship and meet the others back in Molde in the evening."

The invitation was enticing. And they would be doing research along the way. And it would give her a chance to find out more about Conner Holt's connection to the program. How he felt about the others on the team. Not that she wanted to play one off the other, but she needed to see where he "fit" into the scheme of things. What his real connection was with the program. Conner was the proverbial odd man out. She wondered why he was the only climatologist who had been selected to be part of the team.

And on her team.

"As long as the others don't object, or think I'm

shirking my responsibilities, I'd love to join you. As you say, I can gain a bit more information to add to our research."

"Great, it will be good to have company."

Later that afternoon, Brianna joined the two teams in the ship's ample dining area for dinner. They sat around a circular table that accompanied all eight members tucked in a corner so as not to be distracted by the other passengers that were also streaming in for the late afternoon meal. The room was filled with a mixed aroma of spices, coffee, and fresh rolls. Their meal included reindeer served with a currant jelly and goat cheese sauce, with an accompanying helping of Brussels sprouts covered in a savory cranberry sauce. Having had it on her last visit at her aunt's, she knew it was going to be tender and delicious. Apparently, the others didn't seem to either notice or care that they were eating reindeer rather than beef, as they tucked in to their meals. Conversation centered on the ship's amenities, their route along the coast, and their connections with some of the fisheries they planned to visit.

"I understand you and Conner will be heading out on your own when we get to Måløy." Sven drank from his frothy glass, looking between her and Conner. "Deserting the team already?"

"Watch out for the trolls," Bob joked. "I hear they don't take kindly to humans."

"Point taken." Conner smiled and then nodded at Bob in agreement, ignoring Sven's accusation.

The others chuckled, shook their heads, and continued eating.

"Is there a purpose for your deviation?" Sven continued his interrogation.

The rest of the team members' heads bobbed up from their plates, as they all waited to hear Conner's reply. Conner swallowed the last of his meal, drank from his water glass, and directed his gaze at Sven.

Brianna held her breath.

"I want to check out the inner fjords, too. Have something to compare with my coastal findings. Always good to have comparisons when doing research. I promise it won't interfere with your team's research. Or ours, for that matter. We'll meet up with everyone in Molde."

Brianna wasn't sure what Sven was up to, or why Conner felt he had to justify his research methods, but she suddenly became leery of her decision to join him. A decision that was even more doubtful when Sondra offered to tag along.

"I think it's a swell idea," Sondra simpered, batting her eyes at Conner. "I'd love to join you. I hear it's a wonderful touristy destination—a typical flowing mountainous alpine region."

Brianna watched Conner from the corner of her eye. This wasn't the first time Sondra had outright flirted with him in front of everyone. She could only imagine how she acted when she and Conner happened to be alone. He had deflected Sondra's advances several times already. Would he again? She was anxious to see how Conner would handle this in front of everyone. But he didn't have a chance before Lars interjected.

"As leader of your team, you should stay with your group." He spoke with a good dose of authority. "As such, we have a responsibility to be there for our teams." He set his fork on his empty plate and sat back so the server could remove them from the table.

Brianna noticed that no one on Sondra's team championed her defense or commented on the fact that Brianna was the one joining Conner on his off-route excursion. Even Bob held back, despite the smirk on his face.

Sondra's smile, however, disappeared. She looked down at her empty plate, pushed back from the table, and placed her hands in her lap. Brianna felt sorry for the young woman. On the other hand, she knew Sondra was already hot for Conner, and it would have been excruciating having to play third wheel had the woman joined them on this trip. Thankfully, the waiters descended at that moment with a tray full of dessert. Tonight's treat was troll cream, made with fresh lingonberries, served in delicate fluted glass bowls— extremely eye-catching to the senses. Everyone eagerly dug in to their confection, ending the tense air that had encircled the table.

Brianna secretly prayed that this wasn't an omen of how the two teams would interact when they did meet up throughout the next few weeks.

****

Sven couldn't get to his room fast enough after dinner. *Damn it.* What was Conner Holt up to now? And Brianna Murphy? The two of them going off on their own didn't bode well for his operation. What the hell would a climatologist be looking for farther inland when their mission was the coastal waters and Barents Sea? He pulled his cell phone out of his back pocket and punched in Gianni's number. He sat on the edge of the bed and crossed his legs. He counted the number of rings on the other end of the line. "Come on, come on, answer, dammit." The call went to voice mail. "Gianni, give me

47

a call ASAP. There's been a deviation of Team Two's route. I need you to get your men on it right away. Call me." He ended the call and threw his phone on the bed. He jumped up and started pacing the tight quarters, which didn't leave room to vent his frustrations. His phone rang as he was about to head for the shower. He rushed to the bed, picked it up, and checked the caller ID.

"Where the hell have you been?" he shouted at Gianni. "Good God, I'm about ready to have a heart attack wondering what you're up to, let alone questioning what Conner Holt has up his sleeve."

"Hold on. Hold on. I was in conference with one of our contacts," Gianni sputtered. "What's going on there?"

"We have a potential situation that needs probing." He ran his hand over his head, the strands of hair sliding between his fingers.

"What kind of a situation is it that it requires such an urgent call?"

"If you will give me a minute, I'll explain. Our climatologist, Mr. Holt, and a Ms. Murphy are deviating from the original plans. They are going over to the Geiranger area. I don't know what they are up to, but you need to send two of your men to follow them and check it out."

"Is that all the information you have?"

"It's enough. They leave in the morning when we dock in Måløy. I'll text you their vehicle make, model, and license number. They plan to rejoin their group when we get to Molde. Have your men keep an eye on them. See what they're up to. I don't trust them. If anything, we might be able to find something to make them look guilty if it comes to that."

"I know just the two men to send. They are good at ferreting details without being observed. I'll get back to you as soon as I know anything."

"You do that."

If it was the two men he'd seen with Gianni at the top of the Fløien Mountain coffee shop, he had no confidence that they actually knew what they were doing.

Chapter Four

Conner drove their royal-blue SUV down the ship's ramp the following morning when they docked in Måløy. Tourists were off-loading down the gangplank, heading toward two tour buses. Tour managers stood ready to greet the passengers from the ship. And with all the commotion that was taking place, traffic, including them, was blocked. He put the vehicle in park and plugged in the GPS for the location of Lake Eidsdal where a ferry would take them across to the first stop and the start of their day's journey.

Brianna sat across from him, watching the tourists happily make their way onto the bus, no doubt anticipating the day's adventure. "I wonder where they're going?" She beamed, putting on her sunglasses.

"I understand they're heading in the same direction we're heading. Up the mountains to the Trollstigen Pass. We'll more than likely follow the bus to the ferry in Eidsdal that will take us to Linge. Crossing on the ferry will save us a lot of time."

"At least we have a beautiful day for traveling."

"Yes, an exceptionally clear day to traverse the mountains and the Trollstigen Pass." Sitting in the car with Brianna, her excitement shining through her smiling face, warmed his insides. Still, he wasn't sure inviting her to join him had been a good idea. In fact, he didn't know why he had asked her in the first place. He didn't for one minute think she was connected to anything shady, despite her connection to the Kelsey family in Tromsø. And of course, it was an opportunity to try to convince her that global warming was real and that Wild and Wonderful should be made aware of those concerns if they weren't already. The organization had widespread appeal, and people listened to them. Of course, this trip was all business. Nothing personal.

The bus finally moved out. Conner put the SUV in gear and followed at a leisurely pace. There was no rush, and it would give Brianna a chance to enjoy the colorful rural towns and countryside. When they finally arrived in Eidsdal, next to the ferry, Conner let the car idle while they waited in line behind the tour bus and other vehicles waiting to board. Light exhaust fumes engulfed the air. He automatically engaged the controls to make sure the windows were shut.

"Once we're back on the road, we can open them," he said. "It's going to be a warm enough day."

"Not a problem. I don't particularly want to end up with a headache from the fumes."

They sat in silence as they watched cars full of family members, and trucks full of produce or building materials, jockey in position, obviously in a hurry to make sure there was room for them on the ferry before it filled up and the gate closed on them.

"Once on board, we can get out and go up on deck to relax and enjoy the view." Conner kept his eyes on the cars in front of him, making sure he didn't lose his place in line.

"Where do we disembark?" Brianna asked.

"A town called Linge, on the far side of the lake. I've made arrangements to speak to the owner of a small fishery there."

"Are they having trouble with their catch?"

"Not particularly. It's a small operation, but I want to check with them to see if they've noticed any climate changes that are more inland. You can take samples or do whatever research you'd like while we're there. It might prove useful later. Something to compare with your findings along the coast."

"Seeing as our equipment is in the back of the car, I just might. After all, I'm here to work on the project."

"Yes, but in the meantime, we should just relax and enjoy the crossing and the view."

The cars in front of him suddenly moved ahead. Conner joined the queue and prepared to board the ferry. Once onboard, he followed in line and parked the SUV. They waited until the cars behind them had shut their engines down before stepping from their vehicles and securing the locks. Together they joined the crowd and tourists from the bus and climbed the stairway toward the observation deck. Deck chairs lined the edge, diagonally across from the railing.

"Let's head to the far corner of the deck," Conner suggested. "We'll be out of the way of those sitting. Don't want to block their view. Besides, we'll have a better view of the area."

Side by side they walked to the far end of the deck and leaned against the railing. In unison, they looked out over the lake. Lush green forests surrounded the large lake's shoreline in the distance. Several homes nestled in between the trees next to the water's edge gave it a secluded, cozy atmosphere.

"Typical Norwegian scenery." Brianna sighed. "It never disappoints. Somehow it seems soothing, relaxing.

I imagine it's not very different from Alaska."

The sun peeked through the late morning mist, pulling the moisture up into the hillsides and mountains beyond. The morning air was cool. It was going to be a scenic drive through the alpine highlands once they got back on land. The only major distraction he could foresee was having Brianna sitting next to him in such close quarters. All day!

He had to agree. But her being part of his scenery only added to the appeal of the Norwegian countryside. "Actually, I live in Seattle. But I spend a lot of time in Alaska."

He needed to get his mind back on business. He wasn't out here to get involved with anyone, no matter how eye-catching, smart, and delightful they were. He'd invited her on this excursion for business purposes only. And it had to stay that way.

"Wild and Wonderful has an associate that works out of Alaska," Brianna said. "Holly Newman, now Holly Daniels. She married Jake Daniels. She met him while on assignment in Brazil."

"Let me guess, a pipeline deal gone bad?"

"Yes, how do you know about that?" She turned toward him, eyebrows raised.

"We just happen to be acquaintances. I met Jake when I was up there checking out climate change indicators around the Alaskan pipeline. He's a big fisherman. I've gone on a couple of fishing expeditions with him. Alaska is on the same latitude as Greenland and Finnmark here in Norway, by the way."

"So that's why you've been invited to work on this project? Similar climates?"

"Exactly. To determine if there are similar

symptoms here as well. So far, they tend to match. But that's more likely along the coastal waters. Thus, my interest in checking out some of the waterways and the fisheries farther inland."

"At least you have some positive research to compare with your research findings here in Norway. It should help the federation in regard to the possibility of global warming here."

"I hope so." Was she doubting that global warming was real? He was going to have to convince her that it had already had significant implications worldwide. Including the Nordic region.

"So does your family also live in Seattle?"

"No, I live in a duplex apartment building. My family lives in California."

"What? No one waiting for you back in Seattle?"

Her question took him by surprise. He looked out over the lake. They were getting closer to shore, and it would be time to disembark.

"Nope. I'm never in one place long enough to think about settling down. My career takes me around the globe. What about you? Anyone back home waiting for you?" He wasn't sure he should delve into her personal life. After all, it wasn't as if he was interested in forming a relationship with her just because he'd asked her to join him on his sojourn into the fjords.

"Only my parents. In fact, I should give them a call again and see how they're doing. They're recovering from a bad case of influenza. They would love to have joined me while I'm in Norway. Have a family reunion of sorts, but they weren't up to it just yet."

"Sorry to hear. You'd probably get better reception from your cell phone once we reach the other side of the lake."

Before she knew it, they were docking. Conner drove the SUV off the ferry, turned left onto the highway, and headed toward Linge. They made a quick stop at one of the smaller fisheries several miles down the road, then continued to Linge. Linge was a pleasant enough town, but Conner didn't achieve any significant results in regard to climate change. They weren't there long enough for Brianna to do any in-depth research. It was a bit of a disappointment, but on the other hand, she enjoyed interacting with the local fishermen before they moved on to the next fishery on Conner's list. Here they discovered that their small catch was typical for the area, and water samples that she took showed no ill effects in regard to pollutants or the aquatic habitat.

After a short stop at a local café for mid-morning tea, Conner drove their vehicle toward the higher-alpine mountain tops. Starting out with an easy climb, he shifted into second gear and continued toward an overlook where they were able to pull over and check out the cascading waterfalls that plummeted far below into the Geirangerfjord. A long, narrow lake flowed between jutting mountains and glistened in the late morning sunshine. A parking area overlooking the fjord was to the left of the highway. Conner pulled the SUV into an empty spot, close to the edge.

"We can get out and stretch our legs while we take in the view." Not waiting for Brianna to respond, he turned the ignition off and got out of the car.

Brianna didn't hesitate and joined him next to the protective guardrails overlooking the gushing waterfalls and the fjord winding through the valley far below. The water continued its journey and streamed over large boulders along the edges, causing frothy white waves to bounce along the river bed. "I've always wanted to visit this location," Brianna gushed, her arms spread out in front of her. "Just look at it. Isn't it gorgeous? I've heard so much about the Bride's Veil and the Seven Sisters waterfalls. Thanks for giving me the opportunity to finally see them for myself."

"My pleasure." He stood grinning as she proceeded to take several pictures of the falls with her cell phone before tucking it back in her shoulder bag. Other visitors to the site were also taking pictures and leaning over the edge of the deep cliff, aiming their cameras toward the deep fjord.

"There's a visitor center located next to the river up ahead. It has a café. I thought we could stop for lunch." Conner continued to lean over the railing as the two of them took in the view. "It's just down around the bend a bit. We can get a bite to eat and use their facilities before we make our way down the mountainside on the other side to our next stops in the valley below."

"Sounds like a great idea. I am a bit hungry."

Reluctantly, Brianna followed Conner back to their vehicle. The weather was ideal, and she was loath to leave this spectacular setting behind. But this wasn't a vacation, and there were many more scenic sites to enjoy along the way. Still, they had work to do. She climbed into the car, buckled her seat belt, and sighed. She was glad she'd agreed to join him on this impromptu expedition. She couldn't wait to share her memories with her parents when she returned stateside.

Conner leaned out the window to double-check for oncoming traffic before pulling out of the parking area. Finding it clear, he slowly maneuvered the SUV onto the highway. A large, tan-colored van came careening recklessly over the knoll, heading right at them on the wrong side of the road. Conner veered to the right in order to avoid a head-on collision. The oncoming vehicle, instead of correcting its path, swerved directly toward them, their front bumper hitting against the SUV's right back fender. The loud crash twisted their SUV sideways, causing its rear end to bang back against the guardrails, next to the overhang, heading in the opposite direction.

Brianna was thrown against the inside of the door, hitting her shoulder. She screamed, then held her breath, closed her eyes, and hoped the railing was sturdy enough to keep them from careening over the cliff and the mile-high drop-off into the rocky ledge and gushing water far below.

"Shit! Are you all right?" Conner yelled as he tried to regain control of the vehicle and get it turned around.

She held her breath as he quickly surveyed the immediate area. *Oh, my God!* She hoped they hadn't hit someone standing in the overlook area. The damn truck that had caused the accident was nowhere in sight.

He then turned to check the traffic situation again. However, just as he managed to maneuver the car out of the line of traffic, another jolt sent them careening forward, this time swerving onto the highway and into the other lane and oncoming traffic. She sent up a silent prayer that they could get out of the way of the large orange truck that was now heading their way. Conner stepped on the gas, swerved to the side, and thankfully managed to miss the oncoming truck with mere seconds to spare. Obviously, the driver in the other vehicle was paying attention and had stepped on his brakes, narrowly missing a head-on collision with the car. Their own vehicle fishtailed again, causing it to swirl in a 360-degree circle and the rear of their SUV to crash against another series of guardrails before coming to a complete stop. Brianna let out another agonizing scream as her head slammed against the window with a loud thud.

Conner quickly turned the ignition off this time. He rested his head on the steering wheel, his hands tight, his knuckles white. She heard him take in a deep breath before he turned to her.

"Oh, my God. Are you okay? How bad are you hurt?" He released his seat belt and reached for her. He gently wrapped his arm around her shoulders and drew her to him.

"I'm not sure what just happened." She tried to hold back her tears, but they were leaking down her cheeks. "I hit my head on the window. I have a pounding headache. My shoulder is throbbing, too. I hit it up against the door again."

"Can you get your jacket off so I can check to see how bad it is?"

Brianna complied, although her arm was sore. She too wanted to make sure she wasn't seriously injured.

He gently reached for her right arm, rubbed his shaking hand along her shoulder, down toward the elbow. His touch was soothing. But painful in spots.

"I'm pretty sure you'll have a bruise, but I don't think anything is broken. And there is no blood. What about your head? I hope you don't have a concussion. Damn it," he cussed, then leaned over and, without hesitation, planted a kiss on her forehead.

Oh, my God! Did he just kiss me?

His lips were gentle, and she hoped he didn't notice

her body's reaction to his comforting touch. Or was it her nerves from the accident?

He slid back over to the driver's side and gripped the steering wheel. "I can't believe that jerk didn't even stop to see if we were okay. And to be involved in a weird, double crash, one after the other."

"It all happened so fast. You couldn't have foreseen any of this." Brianna's voice trembled. "I hope you don't think I blame you. It was the fault of the man driving the first van. Not yours."

"Give me a minute to check out the damage to the car. Hopefully, it's still drivable, but I want to make sure nothing is severely damaged. The café isn't far from here. Do you think you'll be okay until we get there?"

"Yes."

Conner stepped from the car, only to be surrounded by a handful of bystanders. Brianna heard them ask Conner if they were okay. She didn't hear what Conner told them, but two tall men helped him inspect the SUV for damage.

Brianna sat in the car while they assessed the damage. She reclined the seat, leaned back, and closed her eyes. She needed the time to control her heartbeats after being held in Conner's arms, not to mention the kiss on her forehead. She was beginning to question her decision to accept his invitation to accompany him today—again. If it weren't for those guardrails, she knew she'd be dead. The drop-off over the side of the mountain would have had their car bouncing off the craggy ledge before splatting in the lake far below. It had happened so fast; she hadn't had time to prepare for the impact against the side of the car. Good thing she had had her seat belt on. Her head hurt like hell, but she didn't want Conner to know just how badly her head throbbed. And her shoulder felt like it had come out of its socket, although she was able to move it without much difficulty. But damn, she'd almost lost it when Conner wrapped his arm around her and pulled her close. She had leaned into him, despite the controls between their seats. And she hadn't wanted him to let go.

Conner opened the back of the SUV and inspected their gear. She hadn't given any of the equipment a second thought and hoped it was still in good shape. Unlike her.

She waited until he was back inside before she asked if there was any damage.

"Except for the dented fenders and your indented door, there doesn't seem to be any major damage. It doesn't look as if anything was damaged in the back, either. The equipment seems to be okay. And the car itself seems to be okay." He started the engine and let it idle a few minutes to make sure it was working. "It should be drivable, as I thought." He slowly inched forward.

The two men who had helped him inspect the car stood next to the highway, indicating that it was safe to get back on the road. They waved to him as they left the scenic overlook. He turned the car around and slowly maneuvered back out onto the highway toward their original destination.

"You need to see a doctor as soon as we get to Molde to make sure there aren't any unforeseen injuries or broken bones," he said, keeping his eyes on the road. "Do you think you'll be okay if we stop to get something to eat, as planned?"

"Yes. I could use something to drink as well.

Preferably something stronger than tea." She listened to his soft laugh and couldn't help but smile, too, despite her pain.

"Me, too. If I wasn't driving, I'd join you. But I think, until we find out how badly you're hurt, we should stick with nothing stronger than caffeine."

"Spoilsport."

He chuckled this time.

Ten minutes later he pulled in to the café parking lot. He was out of the car and around the vehicle, opening her door and assisting her before she had a chance to get herself pulled together. She stood for a moment, his hand holding her arm, while she made sure her head wouldn't start spinning once she stood.

"Thanks. I think I'm going to be okay. I'm not dizzy, so I think I can make it."

The concerned look on his face indicated he didn't believe her. He continued to hold on to her as they passed a large, colorful troll in the center of the sidewalk in front of the building. She had to smile at the troll's cuteness, despite its oversized nose and devilish expression. The statue was almost as tall as she was.

"Wait. I need to take a picture of this. Darla will get a kick out of it." She reached into her shoulder bag and retrieved her cell phone with her good arm while Conner stood close by, shaking his head, a smile on his face.

"Who's Darla?" he asked as they entered the restaurant. His wide smile, and charming dimple, on his too-handsome face had her grinning as well.

"One of the ladies back at Wild and Wonderful. She's fascinated with the concept and legend of trolls." She turned to follow him and swayed sideways.

"Come on. You need to sit down." Conner wrapped

his arm around her waist, escorted her inside, and led her to an empty booth.

She slid onto the bench seat and leaned her head against the back of the wooden frame.

"You're looking a little pale. I'll go see if they have something for your headache."

"I have something in my bag. But water would be good." She reached into her shoulder bag while he went in search of water. By the time she dug out a couple of tablets, he was back. She quickly swallowed the over-the-counter pain reliever and then sat back with a deep sigh. She looked across the table and found Conner studying her. He looked as bad as she felt. Although he acted as if the accident hadn't affected him, she could see that it had.

"Are you okay?" she asked. "Did you get hurt, too?" He had appeared levelheaded during the entire ordeal and in control of the vehicle. She'd been so concerned about her own condition that she hadn't given it a second thought that he might have gotten hurt as well. She had been too stunned, and in pain, after being knocked into the side of the car. Twice.

"I'm fine. I'm more concerned about you. You hit your head pretty hard."

"I'm starting to feel better. I'm sure after we get some lunch, and these tablets kick in, I'll be good to go."

A tall, blonde waitress arrived with menus, her smile infectious. They each ordered a soft drink, a crab sandwich, and a bowl of lingonberry soup. Order in hand, the waitress turned and crossed the spacious room toward the bar on the far end.

"Now that I think about it," Conner said, leaning against the table, his hands crossed in front of him, "I'm surprised the man driving the van didn't stop to see if we were okay. He swung back in his lane rather quickly and kept right on going."

"That's exactly what I thought. Do you think he didn't realize he'd forced us off the road? Thank God for the guardrails. They were sturdy enough that we didn't go over the edge." Brianna shivered and rubbed her arm, just thinking about what could have happened had the guardrails not been there. She winced at the pain that shot up her arm from her touch and hoped Conner didn't notice.

"You could be right." He took a long sip from his water glass. "However, it really looked as if he was in control, the way he simply swerved and kept going. It's a wonder he didn't plow into the other vehicles parked in the overlook."

"He didn't seem to be aware of the reaction with the other vehicles behind him, as he nearly killed us."

"Yes, thankfully, no one else was hurt."

Their meal arrived, and together they ate in silence. Afterward, they made a quick trip to the facilities before climbing back into their vehicle for the drive to Molde.

Chapter Five

The Trollstigen Pass soon turned into a descending highway with the sprawling valley of Romsdalsfjord at the foot of the steep mountainside. Brianna looked down from the top of the mountain peak to the valley floor far below. It was wide, level, and covered in lush fields and farmland. But the pass itself leading to the valley was a myriad of thirteen steep, twisting hairpin curves that had Brianna's heart beating a rapid pace. Would their vehicle that had just gone through an accident get them over this pass? In one piece?

Conner took each sharp curve with caution, slowing down in order to stay in his own lane as he maneuvered each bend in the steep road. Almost to the bottom and about to round one of the last two curves, Brianna felt a jolt from behind. She quickly turned to Conner. He was looking through the rearview mirror, a worried frown on his face.

Another loud thunk and a jolt from behind sent her jutting forward. She braced herself against the dashboard and clutched her seat belt.

"Oh, my God! What's going on now?"

"I don't know, but hang on tight."

"This is too ironic. Twice in one day! Do you think someone is out to get us?" She gripped the seat belt tighter, making sure it was secure. Another pain shot up her right arm. If she hadn't already taken something for her headache, she would swallow another pain pill right now. Good Lord, her head throbbed.

"Your guess is as good as mine. Hold tight." Conner's hands tightened on the steering wheel. He looked out the rearview mirror again. "Shit! Hold on. They're coming at us again, and they aren't slowing down."

Brianna braced herself just as another jolt hit from behind and a loud bang echoed in her head. The other vehicle continued to push their SUV, forcing it to skid sideways. Brianna looked out the window and held her breath. There were no guardrails. And it was all downhill. And steep. Thankfully, no drop-offs in this section of the road. The car surged forward. Conner grasped the steering wheel, pumped the brakes, and tried to keep the vehicle on the road. But the vehicle behind them stepped on the gas and pushed against their car. This was no accidental incident this time. It was definitely intentional. She spotted two men inside the truck. Who were these men? What were they after? *And why us?*

Brianna strained her neck and peered out the back window despite her injuries. "Oh, my God, Conner. It's the same van that ran us off the road earlier."

"I see that. What the hell?"

She clasped her hands to her chest, gripped the seat belt, and gasped as the scenery whizzed past the window. "What's going on? What are they trying to do? Why us? Who are they?" She couldn't help repeating.

Conner didn't answer, his full attention trying to keep their car on the road as they approached the next to last hairpin turn at the bottom of the mountain. He was too busy trying to control the car so they wouldn't miss the curve and end up careening down the steep hillside that was covered in brush. Thankfully, the roadway was empty, and he was able to make a wide arc and make it safely around the bend.

She gave a sigh of relief at Conner's ability to keep control of the vehicle. But they weren't so lucky at the last bend in the pass. The large vehicle careened into them from behind, causing Conner to lose control. With sickening speed, their SUV skidded off the road and slid down the steep but thankfully short assortment of field-grass-covered embankment. Luckily, the car remained upright as Conner brought it to a clean stop.

Brianna gasped in shock as their assailant picked up speed and sped on by.

"Are you okay?" Conner asked, eyebrows raised in concern.

"Yes. Thank God!" She leaned back in her seat and shut her eyes.

She heard Conner reach for his cell phone and punch in a number.

Brianna sat still, held her breath, and wondered if they were going to make it back to Molde in one piece. Or at all.

"Lars," Conner practically shouted over the cell phone. "What's going on there? Is everything okay?"

Brianna couldn't hear what Lars said, but apparently it didn't appease Conner.

"We've been run off the road twice already. By the same van. Is everyone there accounted for? Nothing strange happening? No, I don't have any idea who it is. I didn't recognize the man driving. Look, see about renting another SUV for our team. This one is drivable but pretty banged up, as is Brie. We should be there as planned. Arrange for a doctor for Brie. She hit her head and might have a concussion. Her arm is pretty bruised. Thanks. We'll see you later." He turned to her and simply sat across from her, staring.

OMG! Did he just refer to her as Brie? She waited for him to speak, hoping it wasn't bad news.

"We're on our own. Lars said everything is going according to plan at their end. They've stopped at a couple of the fisheries along the way but didn't find anything amiss. Bob hasn't upset anyone lately, and everyone is getting along. Everyone is accounted for."

"At least that's good news. Do you think we aren't the men's intended target? That they've mistaken us for someone else?"

"It crossed my mind. But in any case, like I said, we're on our own. I'm going to head back to Molde without making any more stops along the way. It's an easy route through the valley from here on out. No more mountain passes. We should make good time. I'm ready if you are?"

"As I'll ever be."

"I'm sorry for putting you through this, Brie…"

"Don't go there. None of this is your fault. Whoever this crazy is, we'll be on guard from here on out. I'll help you keep watch."

He nodded, shifted the gears, and maneuvered the SUV back onto the valley highway. They traveled in silence for several miles. The pain in her head was beginning to fade, and her breathing returned to normal. Conner's next words, however, had her nerves jumping.

"What can you tell me about Sven Olson? He seems a rather distant member of the other team."

How to answer? She didn't know much, only what

Bob had implied. "Bob knows him from when he did research on a project in Maine. From what he says, there was a poaching ring in Lobster Cove. Sven was thought to be one of the suspects, seeing as he had family connections in the industry here in Norway. But apparently, nothing came of it."

"Oh? Why is that? What happened to change their minds?"

"For one thing, Bob says that Sven left Lobster Cove with his parents to attend his grandparents' anniversary party. The parents decided to sell their flower shop and join the family fishing business in Bergen. Sven decided to join them and moved to Norway almost immediately. It was at that point that the poaching ring, with ties to the Nordic region, was apprehended."

"Does Bob think Sven is involved in poaching here in Norway?"

"Without coming right out and saying so, I'm sure he does. And wants to prove it."

"Do you think Sven might have had anything to do with our incident?"

"Your guess is as good as mine."

"I'm going to skip the other two stops I had planned. I think it wise we head straight back to the ship and our team. See what's going on there."

Brianna reclined and rested her head on the back of the seat. She turned and looked out the window, then flinched as a pain shot through her neck. Her hand automatically grasped the aching muscle. She sighed and closed her eyes.

"Put the seat back and relax. I'll keep watch as we go. The road along here is much easier to navigate. It's more open. You just hang in there." He reached over and patted her shoulder.

She did as she was told, then watched as he searched the area on either side of the highway and concentrated on driving. If she could only relax and sleep. But her mind continued to reel over their two accidents. Who would have thought their day, which had started out on an adventurous high note, would end up in a confusing conundrum? Thankfully, Conner was levelheaded and had gotten them through their ordeals. Brianna had to give him high marks for his caring demeanor. A warmth spread through her body as she thought of the way he had taken her in his arms. She drew in a deep breath and let it out slowly. Conner Holt was starting to be hard to resist.

It was six o'clock by the time they arrived in Molde. They checked into their designated hotel located on the edge of the seashore.

Lars was there to greet them. "So, Conner, what the hell happened? Any signs of someone following you?"

"No. The rest of the trip was uneventful." Conner related a quick version of their harrowing incidents. "I can fill you in later, but Brie needs to get settled in and relax. Were you able to get a doctor's appointment for her?"

"Sorry. Yes. I contacted the local walk-in clinic. They're open twenty-four seven. You can go as soon as you've checked in."

"Thanks. Is it far from here?" Brianna checked the clock over the reception desk. She had plenty of time to settle in her assigned room and prepare to walk to the clinic.

"It's just down the block and around the corner. You can walk, if you're up to it."

"I'll catch up with you later, Lars. Thanks." Conner took her arm and led her down the hall toward the elevator.

When they reached their appointed rooms on the third floor, Conner inserted the key card to her room. "I'm right next door if you need anything. In the meantime, I'll give you five minutes to pull yourself together. I'll take you to the medical facility to get checked out. I don't think you should be going by yourself."

"Give me ten, and I'll be ready." She watched Conner stride to the room next to hers and insert the key card, then nod to her before entering and closing the door behind him. She was feeling much better, but she wasn't sure she was up to being on her own just yet. Having someone accompany her would ease her mind. Especially if someone was still following them.

The physician's facility was on the first floor. It smelled of antiseptic and cleaning fluids. A receptionist greeted them, checked Brianna in, and then asked them to have a seat while they waited for the physician's assistant to call her. The waiting room was half full with patients waiting to be seen. In the corner was a mother keeping her two young towheaded children busy coloring at a small kid's table. An elderly woman in a wheelchair smiled at her as she and Conner sat in simple, cushioned, wooden armchairs across from her. Other than a triage nurse's booth to the left and a small TV monitor high up on one of the walls, the room was quiet. Brianna expected a long wait but was surprised when the triage nurse called her name. After an initial blood pressure, temperature, and enquiry as to her situation, she was then ushered into a room by a physician's assistant, leaving Conner in the waiting room.

After an initial cognitive exam, requesting Brianna give her name, the current year, where she was, and what happened to her and when, she was given an MRI to rule out any bleeding or bruising of the brain, followed by an x-ray of her arm.

It didn't take long for both results, and the doctor gave her a clean bill of health and a few pain tablets to get her through the night and following day. Relieved, she could only smile as she met Conner back in the waiting room.

"How'd it go?" Conner asked.

"Perfect. Nothing broken. No major head injuries. But I will probably still hurt for a few days. Got some pain meds. Just need a good night's sleep."

"You and me both."

But first they had to get through the evening meal with the combined teams. Something she wasn't looking forward to but didn't want to cancel. She didn't want to give her team the wrong impression of her capabilities once they learned of their mishap and her injuries.

****

Conner and Brianna joined the others in the dining room at the hotel later that evening. A smorgasbord had been set up in a separate room for the fishing federation teams. Brianna scanned the buffet as she walked by and was delighted to find a few of her favorite dishes. Besides herring, there was an assortment of lobster, salmon, stewed veggies over fried fish, lamb and cabbage, a sweet and sour cabbage salad, a carrot and cucumber salad, and fruit compote. Fresh breads filled a basket, and a tray of various cheeses rounded out the spread. Sondra Sølreida approached, zeroing in on

Conner as he was about to help himself to the buffet.

"Lars told us you had an alarming incident today and hit your head. I hope you're okay, Conner?"

All eyes turned their way. Conner glanced at Lars and then turned back to Sondra. Lars shook his head, shrugged his shoulders, and remained silent. Thankfully, Conner took it upon himself to clarify what had taken place before everyone got the wrong idea, saving her from having to do so.

"Brie was the one who was injured. She's the one who hit her head." Conner spoke to the room at large. He stepped back from Sondra, successfully removing her hand from his arm. "In fact," he continued, "Brie was seen by a physician earlier this afternoon when we arrived in Molde. She was given a clean bill of health. There should be no worries as to her continued participation in the project."

Brianna braced herself for a barrage of questions. Was she going to be fit enough to continue her part in the project? Did the accident have anything to do with the project itself?

"Good to hear you're both okay." Bob spoke up from across the large table. He'd obviously already been to the ample buffet. He held up his glass in a toast for their well-being and then continued eating.

"I just need a good night's sleep," she informed them. "Like Conner said, my ability to keep up with everyone and maintain my level of research will not be hampered. So there is no need to worry."

"What about you, Conner?" Sondra asked, concern etched on her lovely face, as she stepped closer to him again. "Didn't you get hurt as well?" She grasped his arm.

Sondra's concerned expression wasn't lost on Brianna. Nor on Conner, if she read his resigned expression correctly.

"I wasn't hurt, but it was a stressful day for both of us." He stepped toward the buffet and picked up a plate, disengaging Sondra's hand from his arm. "I'm looking forward to a good meal and a good night's sleep as well."

Brianna quickly stepped forward as Conner handed her a plate, silently indicating she should get in line to help herself. He followed behind her as she went through the line, both of them helping themselves to several of the many delicious appetizing dishes.

"I've saved a seat for you over here, Conner."

Sondra's pleading tone and sultry words grated on Brianna's nerves when the woman didn't let up. Sondra pointed to the empty chair next to where she had been sitting.

Stefan Dutlov, seated on the other side of Sondra, was obviously annoyed with Sondra's display. The man's disgruntled look, his mouth a tight, pinched line, left little to the imagination as to his stance on Sondra's affection for Conner. It was more than obvious he was smitten with the woman. Not at all happy with her obvious flirtations with Conner. Conner took it all in stride, however, and sat in the chair Sondra had indicated. Which left Brianna to sit in the chair next to Ivan Alexander, the Russian on their team.

Sven acknowledged their presence the minute they sat down at the table. "So, Conner, except for your little mishap, how did your research go? Find any signs of climate change along the Trollstigen Pass waterways? Weren't you checking out some of the fisheries next to the Romsdalsfjord Valley as well?"

Brianna wasn't sure where Sven was going with his questions. And to dismiss it as a "little mishap." Had Conner told the Norwegian where they were going? What fisheries they were going to check out? After their accident she was starting to question everything. Everyone. Including the accident—if it was an accident. And especially Sven.

"We decided to make our way back to Molde to get medical attention for Brie first," Conner told them. "We skipped our visits to the two fisheries I had intended to call on. Brie's health was more important. I can always visit the area another time."

"I hope it hasn't hindered your research here in Norway?" Sven continued, eyebrows raised.

"Not in the least. What about you? What progress has your team had today?"

Sondra spoke up before Sven could answer. "We had an excellent day touring one of the main fish factories." As leader of her team, she swiftly proffered an "in charge" persona. "One of the large trawlers was docking when we arrived. We were able to be on hand when they off-loaded their catch to the factory for processing. The catch was satisfactory, so there was no reason to do further research in the area."

"There was another trawler in the distance," Stefan added. "We were told it's a freezer trawler with capabilities to process and freeze the fish before delivery. They weren't expected in port for another day or two."

"Do you think it might be involved in piracy?" Bob scanned those seated around the table. "I understand there are those who have strong economic incentives to cash in on international markets?"

What the hell was Bob up to now? Was he digging for information? Someone to trip up and hopefully unintentionally give themselves away? Brianna looked over at Conner, who was directing his gaze at each of the team members before settling on Sven again—who was ignoring the question and busy eating.

But Bob didn't let it go. "I'm just saying. If we're here to research why the catch is so low in many places around the coast, then we should be aware that there might be other reasons causing the decline."

"I'm sure the authorities will handle that aspect of the situation," Conner said. "Especially if there are any noticeable indications of such a case. In the meantime, we need to focus on our assigned mission."

"I agree with Conner," Sondra stated. "We each have our own goals from here on out. I suggest we focus on them."

The others nodded in agreement. Brianna was going to have a talk with Bob about his antagonistic approach before the teams separated and moved on. His caustic comments certainly hadn't paved the way for a smooth, friendly, joint quest. Unfortunately, she wasn't going to be able to keep a watch on him, as he was on the other team. She shuddered, virtually shook her head, picked up her glass of tea, and took a long satisfying sip. She really did need something stronger. But with the medicine she was prescribed, alcohol was out of the question for the next few days.

"There's a bar just around the corner." Lars stood, placed his napkin on the table, and smiled at the group. Had he read her mind? "Anyone care to join me for a nightcap?"

Several pushed back from the table to join him.

Brianna declined.

"I'll see Brianna to her room first," Conner stated. Without waiting for their reactions, he came to her side and escorted her from the dining hall.

"Really, Conner. I can make it to my room on my own."

"No arguing, Brie. I can see how tired you are. You must still be hurting. How's the head?"

"I'm ready to cave. But you didn't need to escort me. You can go join the others. I'm sure Sondra will be waiting." She couldn't help the grin that spread across her face.

He looked at her and grimaced. "She can wait all she wants. I'm not interested, in case you haven't noticed. Besides, I want to make sure you make it to your room without incident."

"And that means…what? Am I in danger?"

"That remains to be seen. Just taking precautions. My room is right next to yours. As I said, I'll be right next door if you need anything."

"Thanks, but once I take these pain meds the doctor gave me, I'll be out like a light." Knowing Conner would be next door in case she did need assistance was comforting.

"Ask for a wake-up call for seven o'clock. I'll knock on your door at seven thirty, and we can go down to breakfast together."

Before she knew it, he took the key card from her hand, inserted it in the door, opened it, gave her a quick hug, a kiss on her forehead, nudged her inside, and shut the door behind her. The fact that he literally shoved her inside and shut the door didn't bother her as much as his firm, comforting hug and another kiss on her forehead. It was a good thing she had pain pills to help her sleep; otherwise, she'd be lying awake all night thinking about the hug—and the two kisses on her forehead. And Conner Holt.

****

The darkened, noisy bar was in full swing when Conner entered. He spotted the group at a table in the far corner of the crowded room. He ordered a drink from the bar and carried it over to the table where Lars, Bob, Stefan, and Sondra had already gathered. He settled on the stool between Lars and Stefan. He was surprised and a bit disappointed that Sven and Ivan hadn't joined them. He'd been hoping to find out more about each of their backgrounds and research going forward. He was beginning to suspect things weren't as they appeared on the surface. Accident aside, he didn't anticipate those on the two teams were involved in foul play. But he'd been proven wrong before, and it paid to pay attention.

"Glad you could make it, Conner. How is Brianna doing?" Bob asked. "Are you sure she's going to be okay?"

"Doc said she's fine, just needs rest. What about you, Bob? You ready for tomorrow's visits? I hear there's an inoculation session on the schedule. Your team is checking it out, right?" Conner tried to shift the conversation back to their assignments.

"Yes, although I've seen this setup several times. The fish are placed in tanks, then taken out one by one and inoculated and thrown into a separate tank filled with clean water before they're returned to the fish-farm area. A rather boring operation."

"Yes, but a necessary one for the health of the fish." Lars spoke up. "The federation insisted several of the operations along this coastal area be checked out to make sure there are no contaminants being passed along from tank to tank, possibly causing the decline." He turned to Conner. "We're scheduled to visit one in Tromsø, the Kelseys, if I'm not mistaken."

"I'm familiar with the one in question." Ivan joined the conversation. "I can vouch for them. They run a clean operation."

"Still, it's best to do a thorough check." Bob lifted his glass of beer and took a long draw.

The others followed suit, which allowed Conner to change the subject to more mundane topics. He was starting to use Brianna's tactics when it came to smoothing over Bob's sarcastic barbs. What was with that guy, anyway? Were the man's caustic jabs a technique to dig for information, hoping someone would slip up and reveal…what? Did Bob think someone on the team, other than Sven, was involved in wrongdoing? Didn't he know that everyone on both teams had been vetted by the federation? Was the federation really looking into climate change, or was he being used as a decoy? It hadn't gone without notice that he was the only climatologist on either team. He almost wished Bob was on his team so he could keep an eye on him. And dig deeper into the man's mindset.

****

"You better tell me that you were able to move your catch farther out to sea and as far away from the coast as possible." Cell phone to his ear, Sven paced toward the window. He hadn't anticipated Gianni's men actually causing an accident and hurting someone so close to the teams, even if it was Team Two. He stopped to look out the hotel window at the night sky. Land of the midnight sun be damned. He still wasn't used to the long daylight hours since returning to Norway.

"Right. With him and his girlfriend out of commission and headed back to Molde, we took stock, loaded up, and then went inland a bit before circling back toward Bergen." Gianni's voice was explicit.

"Good. Good. We've managed to finish with research up along the seaboard on our way to Tromsø. You can go back to Molde and regroup. Your contact is waiting offshore, past the main harbor."

"Wasn't the vessel questioned?"

"No. They were assured that it was just a holding refrigeration vessel that had already registered their catch. Besides, I don't think they're looking for anything other than what the federation has assigned them to investigate, but it doesn't hurt to keep an eye out."

"What about that fella from Wild and Wonderful? The one you know from Maine? The one on your team?"

"Nah, he's just your typical argumentative American. No worries there," Sven assured him.

"What about Tromsø?"

"What about Tromsø?" What was Gianni up to now? Sven was beginning to wonder if he could trust the man.

"Isn't that where you'll all meet up again in a couple of days?"

"Yes, so send a couple boats up that way to keep an eye on things. If you find anything amiss, deal with it. But keep my name out of it and try not to maim anyone in the process this time."

"Hey, it kept them away from the area our men were in, didn't it?"

"Right. But we don't want blood on our hands, so be

careful this time."

"Make sure you don't mess up as well. I don't trust that Bob fellow. From what I hear, he's on a mission from back east. Do you think he's on your tail? Digging for dirt that might implicate you?"

Sven didn't know where Gianni had gotten his information in regard to Bob, but it wasn't a bad idea to keep a close watch on the man. Having him on his team had been a good idea, but now he wasn't so sure. He'd have to watch his step. Try to placate the man. Make it look as if his connection to the federation was on the up and up.

Chapter Six

Brianna sat in the back seat with Conner while Ivan drove the SUV up and around Molde's Alps of Summore, heading toward Tromsø. Lars was in the front passenger seat. After their mishap going through the Geirangerfjord the other day, she found it hard to relax, especially with the low shoulder and mile-high drop-offs on her side of the road. Although the morning had started out on a good note, the silence in the car was heavy, due to Bob once again stirring up a hornet's nest over breakfast with accusations of possible foul play in regard to the decline in reported catch. Conner had remained silent as Bob continued to intimate that climate change had no part in the situation along the Norwegian coastline, and therefore it wasn't necessary to have someone make up facts that weren't realistic.

The team had visited several of the local salmon hubs after breakfast. Although the town itself was known for its administrative and trade center, as well as being a tourist town, they had found nothing significant to report, had checked out of their hotel, and decided to get an early start for the long drive up the coast toward Tromsø.

Brianna was looking forward to visiting with her aunt and uncle later that evening. She hoped to get an inside perspective of her uncle Bjorn's operations ahead of the team's official visit the following day. And to visit with her cousin, Kristina. In the meantime, she took advantage of the solitude in the car and rested her head on the back of the seat. Having had a good night's sleep and taken another pain tablet, she was pleased to report that she wasn't feeling any major side effects from yesterday's incident. The pain medication had taken care of that. Still, she shut her eyes, only to wake an hour later to find herself nestled in Conner's arms. She tried to sit upright, but his solid arm around her shoulders held her in place.

"Relax. You needed your rest. How's your head and shoulder?"

"Still a bit sore, but not uncomfortably so. I'll be fine."

He pulled her closer. She tilted her head back on his chest, but she couldn't relax. This close to Conner Holt was a mistake. Being held in his arms was wrong. It felt…warm, comforting…right. He was a strikingly handsome man with a kind heart. But she couldn't let these feelings grow into something that would never come to fruition. They were worlds apart, and a long-distance relationship would never work—or last, as he had also indicated. So why was she wrapped up in his arms?

Crap! She had a job to do, and she had to keep her mind on the project. Especially if her uncle was involved in a black-market scheme. Good Lord. She hoped that wasn't the case. She hated that Bob had intimated there was a connection. She couldn't get it out of her head.

She pulled out of Conner's arms, rubbed her hands over her face, and stared out the side window. Anywhere but at Conner. What she saw as she looked out the window had her turning back around and shutting her eyes. The scenery itself was dramatic, breathtaking, but she wasn't fond of heights after their episode in Geiranger. Now the twisting road with the mile-high drop-off had her heart racing. Like the first half of their drive, the remainder of their trip to Tromsø was accomplished in an even heavier silence.

She was glad when they finally arrived at their hotel midafternoon. Ivan parked the SUV in an empty space next to the three-storied building hugging the bay. They all stepped out into a picture-perfect Norwegian postcard scene. Beside the row of colorful historic buildings lining the street, a series of docks hugged the coastline opposite, and the boardwalk was bustling with activity. Thankfully, Brianna had worn her sunglasses, as the reflection from the sun on the clear aqua water was close to blinding and giving her another headache.

She joined the men, now dealing with their overnight bags, lifted her own, and together they entered the hotel, signed in, and were escorted to their rooms.

"With the evening free tonight, I plan to get a taxi and go visit my cousin," she addressed the three men as they boarded the elevator to the third floor. "Perhaps I can encourage my uncle to take us out on his trawler tomorrow so we can check out the seabed."

"That's a great idea." Lars nodded. "Give me a call when you get back tonight and let me know what you've arranged. The other team should be arriving in town before long, if they haven't already. We'll meet up with them at some point. Although their assignments here are different than ours."

The elevator stopped, the door swished open, and the team stepped out into the hall behind her. Conner followed her down the corridor, to the right, while Lars and Ivan turned to the left. After being held in Conner's strong arms during their long drive, she wasn't sure how she felt about his room being next to hers. Again. Especially as he once again suggested she knock on his door if she needed anything.

****

Brianna twirled a long strand of hair between her fingers, her elbows planted firmly on the kitchen table. She sat across from her cousin, Kristina, who had met her at the door with open arms and condolences for her parents' illness. Now Brianna cradled her teacup in her right hand as she looked out the kitchen window at the picturesque hillside overlooking the cool evening waters of the fjord below. *Aaahh*, the good times she'd had as a child, visiting the Kelseys with her parents. Contemplating the questionable cloud hanging over her uncle's fishing operations cut in on her fond memories. She had to believe that they weren't involved in any way.

The Kelsey fishing trawlers were docked down below, their massive operation and buildings snuggled along the harbor. Streetlights shone off the waters around her uncle's vessels, and the heavy sea mist wafted through the open window over the kitchen sink. She wished she felt more at peace, but keeping her mission to herself was imperative. And the accidents that she and Conner had been involved in. She had to feel Kristina out first, find out what she knew. If her cousin knew anything relevant.

"So what really brings you to Tromsø?" her cousin suddenly blurted. "I hear the federation is conducting an all-out effort to determine the cause of the reduction in catch, even if it isn't due to climate change. And climate change? Really? I hope they don't think we're up to no good. I understand from *Far*, Father, that ours is one of the fishing operations under scrutiny. As if we weren't reporting all our catch."

The scenic relaxing ambiance ended by her cousin's negative and disbelieving caustic words had her quickly swallowing her tea and replacing her cup in its saucer. Obviously, Kristina had heard the rumors, too. She hadn't been aware her family knew they were being watched. Before she could reply, Kristina continued.

"Really, Brianna, what does your team think they are going to find by inspecting *Far's* operations? As for climate change? I don't think it's a problem." Kristina raised her hands in the air, her blonde hair swirling around her face as she shook her head from side to side, and then slapped her hands on the table, jarring the teacups and saucers. "What does the climate have to do with anything? Least of all a decline in fish? Besides, our catch is just about normal."

Kristina's rant took Brianna by surprise and out of her emotional sense of homecoming. She sat back and stared at her cousin in dismay. Kristina's attitude seemed a tad off-key. Kristina was usually a bubbly, devil-may-care person. But her cousin's assumption that the team was looking to find something wrong with their family operation was too close to the truth. If there was a trail of wrongdoing here in Tromsø, she hoped it had nothing to do with the Kelseys' fishing operation.

"Like the situation has anything to do with global warming," Kristina continued. "What does global warming have to do with fishing in the Barents Sea, anyway? Besides, isn't this Conner person only a weatherman, not a marine biologist like you?"

Try as she might, Brianna couldn't dispel the fact that her cousin's defenses were firmly in place. She didn't blame her. On the other hand, she couldn't let it go.

"The entire team is open to all possibilities, Kris. Conner Holt isn't the only one on this fact-finding mission. The team is comprised of Russians, Americans, and Norwegians, with their individual expertise in regard to this situation. Actually, I'm surprised you don't know Sven Olson, Sondra Sølreida, or Lars Jensen—they are all from the federation. I'm sure your father is familiar with them."

Kristina sat back as if chastised. Brianna smiled at her cousin, hoping to relieve the tension that surrounded them in the cozy family kitchen. She really didn't want their first visit to set a negative tone for the rest of her time in Tromsø. They had always gotten along so well during her family's visits when growing up. She wanted to keep it that way.

"I've heard *Far* mention Sven's name many times, but not the others. Good to know he's on the team. *Far* speaks highly of him."

Brianna wasn't going to share her own concerns in regard to Sven Olson's connection with the incident back in Lobster Cove. But it was a tidbit of information she couldn't shake. Especially after what she and Conner had been through on their Geiranger expedition. And thanks to Bob's innuendoes that something was amiss, which had nothing to do with climate change. She was beginning to seriously consider that Sven might be involved, even though there was no proof. *Yet.* Maybe she should delve deeper into Bob's innuendoes. Find out what the connection was between Sven Olson and the Kelseys' operation. Was it personal? Or strictly business?

"Yes, well, how about we take a deep breath and start over?" Brianna waited while Kristina did just that before she continued. Wanting to delve into the connection with Sven, she decided to hold off and change the focus of their conversation. "For one thing, Conner Holt is not just a weatherman. He's a highly respected climatologist, having done extensive research on global warming. Which, I might add, affects every living species on the planet. Haven't you heard about the droughts and wildfires in major areas in California and even Australia? And the heavy flooding, unseasonal storms everywhere? Why, even over here the weather has affected crops. So why not the fishing industry?" She couldn't believe she was sticking up for Conner. Regardless, facts were facts. He was a well-respected climatologist. And he was beginning to convince her that there was an aspect of climate change involved. Her opinion of him had nothing to do with the fact that she was beginning to like him. A lot.

"Point taken," Kristina admitted. "But *Far's* catch hasn't been affected to the degree that we're hurting. We're still a solvent fishing operation."

"Glad to hear Uncle Bjorn's company is doing well. However, the Norwegian Fishing Federation must think they are onto something if they've contacted the American Global Warming Consortium and Wild and Wonderful to help them determine if it is global warming causing the decline in catch, especially cod, or something else. I'll be taking water samples and combing the ocean floor tomorrow to see what else I might find. Hopefully, Uncle Bjorn will take us out on his vessel."

"I'm sure he will agree. I do understand there are a couple outfits farther north who are starting to see a dip in catch along the Barents Sea," Kristina relented. "But it's sporadic and hasn't affected their bottom line yet. Now, I've heard that king crab is another matter. Maybe you all should be checking them out."

"I'm sure we will." Brianna sat back and sipped her tea, relieved Kristina had gotten over her initial angst and was rethinking the situation and even giving her leads farther north. She had hoped her Norwegian family, owners of one of the largest fishing companies in Norway, would be a willing partner in helping with the investigation and not part of the problem. She couldn't wait to talk to her uncle.

"There is always a possibility something else is going on," Brianna confided. "That's why the consortium contacted Wild and Wonderful Incorporated. As you know, they work hand in hand with other entities when it comes to these types of fact-finding missions. I was happy to sign on, seeing as I have strong family ties here in Norway." Brianna grinned at Kristina across the table. "A family connected to the fishing industry. It was the perfect opportunity to reconnect with you, seeing as it's been several years since I came for a visit. And, like I said, I was hoping Uncle Bjorn could accommodate us and take us out on one of his ships."

"Yes, I'm sure *Far* will be happy to accommodate your team. In fact, I think he mentioned that it was already arranged. Wish I could join you, but I have daycare duties at the church's preschool this week. Are you busy this evening? Do you have time to have dinner with us tonight? *Mor*, Mother, is excited about your visit and is shopping at the fish market, hoping you'd join us."

"Wouldn't miss it. Can't wait to see Uncle Bjorn and Aunt Anna."

She was relieved Kristina changed the subject. She didn't want to confirm her cousin's assumption of why she had signed on to the Arctic Project. However, her cousin mentioning Sven's name had raised a red flag. She had talked to Bob before they left for Tromsø, and he had reiterated that he was part of the team that had uncovered a fraudulent fishing outfit that had been stealing from others along the Atlantic coast in Maine. The outfit had strong ties to several Norwegian and Russian outfits—fisheries whose catches had also drastically dwindled in recent months along the Barents Sea. But the news that Sven Olson's name had been connected with her family's operation had been a surprise. Once again, she prayed they weren't involved in anything shady.

She rubbed her forehead. The stress of her conversation with Kristina, and the concerns over her family's possible connection to a black-market operation, had brought on a headache. It was time to head back to the hotel, take another dose of pain medication, and rest. Not the way she had envisioned her afternoon. On the other hand, if she was to return to enjoy dinner with her family, she could use a bit of quiet time.

Dinner later that evening consisted of her family's traditional creamy potato salad, cod, an assortment of fresh vegetables, and a warm family welcome. Headache gone and fully restored after a nap, she enjoyed catching up on family events. Her Uncle Bjorn and Aunt Anna, both in their fifties and hearty but not overly stout, had greeted her with open arms. Kristina, back to her bubbly self, had helped her mother in the kitchen before they all sat down to eat.

"I'm so sorry to hear about your parents." Aunt

Anna frowned, fork in hand as she leaned toward Brianna across the table. "I was so hoping they would be able to join us once I heard you were coming."

"They feel bad but wanted me to let you know they plan on visiting soon."

"We are sorry that your visit is work-related, not simply an opportunity to spend more time with us," Uncle Bjorn interjected. "We would have called the others together for a mini family reunion. However, I have arranged to take your team out on our morning fishing trip. It will give your team an idea of how we operate."

"Thanks so much, Uncle Bjorn. I'm sure they'll appreciate the opportunity to see it all firsthand." She wanted to ask her uncle about Sven Olson's connection to his business but bit her tongue. She held back, not wanting to disrupt this warm family gathering her first night in Tromsø. After tea and dessert—her favorite troll cream with lingonberries—she offered to help clean up, but her aunt refused her help and sent her on her way.

"You have an early morning if you are going out with the crew tomorrow. You will need your rest. We will see you again before you leave town."

Hugs and kisses followed. Brianna left in a cloud of comforting warmth that got her through the night.

****

Brianna's right arm protested the minute she rolled out of bed and put pressure on it the following morning. A sinus headache had woken her. At least she hoped it was only her sinuses that was causing the headache. She really didn't want to take any pain medication today, but there was no way she'd make it until noon without something to alleviate the pain. Going out on the water this morning with her uncle's crew was important to the team's research. She needed to be in top form, especially if she planned to dive.

She padded barefoot over to the small window overlooking the waterfront and pulled the curtain aside. No wonder her head felt as if it weighed a ton. The entire Tromsø harbor was fogged in. It was going to be a typical damp, foggy, rainy Norwegian morning.

She stumbled to the bathroom and fought with the medicine container that stood next to the sink. The small white pill slipped from her fingers and rolled across the countertop. She caught it just before it slipped into the sink and disappeared down the drain. Using the paper cup from the side dispenser, she filled it with water and swallowed the bitter pill. She dressed for a day out on the ocean, grabbed her rain gear, her backpack, and made her way down to the hotel restaurant to meet the others for breakfast. Both teams were in town, although they were investigating separate fishing operations before moving on.

"With this heavy fog, I suggest we postpone sailing out this morning," Bob was grumbling when she reached their table. "Can't see a damn thing out there. I for one could use the time to check out the operations on land while we have the chance."

"Haven't you heard? We have top-notch navigational equipment on board these days," Lars pointed out. "We can sail right through fog without a mishap. I assure you no one will bump into anything along the way."

A few snickers came from the others at the table. Brianna noticed Conner refrained and continued to sip his coffee. But she didn't miss the smile he tried to hide behind the napkin he used to wipe his mouth. Despite a slight headache this morning, she couldn't help but smile as well and followed Conner's lead and sipped from her coffee cup. As did Stefan and Ivan. Sven and Sondra were absent this morning.

Lars scanned the occupants around the table, nodded to Conner, and announced, "Team Two will meet at the main dock in half an hour. Mr. Kelsey will meet us there to give us a quick rundown of his operation. I assume you all have your assignments for the morning. I'll see you then." He pushed his chair back from the table, stood, gave eye contact to his team, and left the restaurant.

The morning wasn't off to a good start, that was for sure. Hopefully, the pain meds would kick in over breakfast so she could deal with having to investigate her family's business and hope they weren't involved.

Conner stood on the dock next to his teammates as Brianna's uncle walked along the quay and met them at the gangplank. He'd done a bit of research on the Kelseys' operation the night before while everyone else went their separate ways. The Kelseys looked legit, but their catch was down, just like the other fisheries. He hoped it wasn't due to Brianna's uncle not reporting it correctly, as reports of others having done so in a few of the more northern locations up along the coast. The reason for not reporting was purported to be due to the black market. Something Bob Wilkins had been intimating from the start. But it was obvious climate change had played a hand in the conditions here in Norway as well. That could be a major force in the cause of the decline in fish. Convincing others was going to be a hard sell.

Bjorn Kelsey and two of his crew greeted them as they approached the large fishing vessel. Conner could see the crew members were already up on deck, making sure the vessel was fully equipped, organized, and ready for launch.

"Welcome. If you're ready, we can board and set sail." Bjorn offered his hand in greeting. "You'll notice we aren't taking the side fishing nets on our excursion today. It would slow us down. My men, Henry and Franklin, will be on hand to assist you. If you have any questions, feel free to check with one of them. They will give you a brief tour of the ship, and then I will meet you up on deck when you're finished."

Bjorn looked at Brianna and winked, then stepped aside so the team could board. Conner took this as an affectionate sign toward his niece, without making a big to-do over her being his relative and a member of the team who would be inspecting his business.

Henry and Franklin, two tall but sea-worthy-looking young men, seemed eager to escort them. Their smiles a sign that they enjoyed their work and seemed to be on friendly terms with Mr. Kelsey. After shaking hands with the team, the two men escorted the team aboard the fishing vessel. Conner held back as the others preceded him up the gangway.

The fishing trawler was a standard, mid-sized ship with two levels. A quick inspection of the vessel confirmed that the operation was top notch. With a fish room on the lower level to inoculate the fish, ponds on the upper deck to transport their catch, both toward the bow, it was large enough to handle an impressive haul and keep the fish alive until they returned to port. Nothing seemed out of order. Conner knew Lars would be checking Mr. Kelsey's record of catch, but as that wasn't part of his specific connection to the project, he decided to remain up on deck, hoping the fog would lift as the morning progressed.

An hour later, Conner was glad he had worn a warm waterproof jacket against the wetness of the heavy fog. He was ready to find a cup of coffee and a place to dry off. Just as he turned to head to the galley, the remainder of his teammates appeared. Mr. Kelsey joined them and led the way to the galley.

"Grab a cup of coffee or tea. There are some scones as well. We'll take them all with us to my quarters. There is plenty of room there where we can talk."

The office was spacious, nautical, and organized. On the port side, a Victorian secretary desk of walnut stood next to the oval window, polished to perfection. Despite its obvious age, it was in excellent shape. And, without a doubt, a sign of the company's wealth. Hopefully, the wealth wasn't from some underhanded scheme, as Bob was constantly implying.

Bjorn Kelsey opened the top center drawer, pulled out a leather-bound notebook, turned, and indicated that everyone should have a seat. As soon as everyone pulled out a white ladder-back cushioned chair and made themselves comfortable, their coffee and scones placed on the matching conference table, Bjorn sat, opened his ship's diary, and faced them.

"I want to assure you that according to my records, I have noticed the signs of global warming in the area," Bjorn informed them, facing Conner. "And yes, our overall catch is lower than normal. And before you ask, there has been some suspicious activity in the area. A couple of vessels we've never seen before have moored closer to our shores but have kept a distance for a day or two and then moved on."

"Is that unusual?" Lars enquired. "Could they just be ships passing through?"

"Most ships that pass through don't linger. They don't come ashore for long periods of time. Now, cruise ships and tourists are different. We are always made aware of these tours. What we have been seeing is a handful of dubious-looking men wandering the streets and frequenting several of the local pubs."

"Have there been any incidents that indicate they are troublemakers, roughhousing men, or criminals?" Ivan Alexander asked, saving Conner from enquiring.

"So far, no. The police are keeping watch, but so far no one has reported any complaints."

"What about the water temperature? The level of algae, the ocean floor?" Brianna asked her uncle. "As you know, I'm planning to dive while we go out today. Make sure there isn't something out there that could be causing the fish to develop serious illnesses. I hear talk of parasites that have been affecting the fish."

"Possible," her uncle said. "It will be great if you would check for any parasites or other conditions that might be causing a problem while you are down below."

Conner backed her decision. "I would like to go along with you on the dive. It will give me a chance to see what the undersea reveals in regard to climate change in this area. Something to compare with the region farther north."

"What about the other team?" Ivan looked at Lars, then Bjorn. "I understand from Sondra that they are scheduled to dive here in Tromsø, too. Is it necessary for us to do so as well? Isn't that redundant?"

"That's the point," Lars explained. "We'll have two sets of opinions to either question our findings or agree with them. They are with another fishing fleet today. As I understand it, Mr. Kelsey is taking us north, along his coastline, this morning to do our research." He looked at Bjorn for confirmation.

The man nodded.

Lars continued. "In fact, they are heading on up the coast later this afternoon. As we're staying in Tromsø another day, we won't see them again until we meet up at the North Cape later in the week."

"So, in the meantime, relax," Bjorn encouraged. "I will let you enjoy your tea while I go make sure our captain and crew have everything in order for your dive. I will meet you up on deck in half an hour."

Was Brianna's uncle mentioning a possible black-market operation his way of detracting from their connection? Or simply a sharing of his concerns with the team?

Chapter Seven

Brianna had been on her uncle's vessel during her last visit, five years ago. But this time it wasn't a joyride with her cousin, Kristina. This time it was all business. Brianna stood starboard on the upper deck and looked out at the heavy fog. The fresh scent of ocean helped to calm her mixed emotions in regard to today's mission. She took in a deep breath, held it a minute, then let it out slowly and evenly. Dressed in her wet suit, she pulled her hair back in a ponytail and then adjusted her water goggles and air tank in preparation for her dive.

Her uncle, standing beside her, gave her the thumbs-up as she proceeded to walk to the side of the ship and step up on the platform. Conner stepped forward, ready to accompany her, fully outfitted as well.

"You didn't think I'd let you go down below by yourself, did you?"

His smile disarming, she could only nod her approval.

"Like I said, I'd like to check out the ocean floor as well. You never know what it might reveal—climate change-wise, of course. You're the expert in other matters."

"I'm glad to have company, thanks."

"I know you do this for a living," her uncle said, "but I feel much better knowing there's someone down there with you."

"Thanks, Uncle Bjorn. I'll be fine. I do this for a living, as you said." She faced Conner. "Ready to do this?"

"After you."

His grin was heart-warming. For whatever reason, she was more comfortable having someone, especially Conner, go down below with her this time. With all the worry about black markets, innuendoes of connections within the teams, not to mention their previous incidents, it was reassuring to have company. And to have Conner be the one to accompany her added an ounce of security she hadn't felt she needed on other dives.

This one felt different.

Conner held out his hand. She slid hers into his strong hold without hesitation. They locked eyes, smiled, then nodded they were ready. The ship suddenly pitched from side to side, dipping then rising out of the water. Hand in hand they lost their footing and tumbled backward into the churning Arctic waters. Brianna's hand slipped from Conner's, and they sank into the depths of the ocean as the side of the ship tilted, rose again, took a sharp, deep dip, and slapped back in place. Gushing waves pushed her deeper and farther away from the boat. And Conner. Unable to ascertain her coordinates, due to the height of the waves obscuring her whereabouts, she was sucked back under once again before she was able to finally gain control. She paddled her fin-laden feet, propelling her to the surface. Her breath coming in gasps, she splayed her hands to the sides above the water to hold her in place. She searched for Conner, only to find him several yards to her left, scanning the perimeter through the mist. Before she could think about swimming to his side, she lost her momentum as another giant wave rocked against the boat, splashed back in her direction, pushed her farther out to sea, and pulled her back under. She struggled underwater, trying to re-attach her oxygen mask, only to bob up to the surface once again. She swiftly swam away from the ship in order to escape getting caught in another backwash caused by the surge so she wouldn't be drawn in and up against the boat. She turned to assess her situation and came face-to-face with Conner. His arms reached for and encircled her. She gratefully wrapped her arms around him, and together they treaded water, waiting for the waves to calm.

"What just happened?" she shouted, lifting her mask, looking back at the ship, now steady as if nothing had happened.

"I have no idea, but I'm going to find out. This can't be another accidental mishap. Come on, the boat looks like it's settled. Let's get back on board and find out what the hell just happened."

Brianna kept pace with Conner, now that the ocean's waves had settled, and together they swam back to her uncle's trawler. Henry and Franklin were standing on deck, looking out to sea with their telescopes. Spotting them, both pointing in their direction. The two men sent up a signal indicating they'd been found. When she and Conner finally reached the ladder attached to the side of the ship, Henry reached over and gave them a hand up into the craft.

Once on board, totally out of breath and still perplexed over the whole incident, Brianna let the men help her remove her heavy equipment so she could sit on the bench and catch her breath. Conner, instead, stood and confronted the two men.

"What the hell just happened?" he shouted. "Where is everyone?"

Brianna noticed they were the only two up on deck. Where were the others? Uncle Bjorn? The rest of the team?

"Where is everyone?" she repeated Conner's question, standing on wobbly legs. "What is going on?"

"Apparently, a smaller boat got lost in the fog and sailed right into the side of us," Henry said, running his hand through his thin hair as his feet danced from side to side. "Bjorn is checking with everyone to see if anything is amiss. See if there is any damage. He sent us up to keep an eye out for the two of you."

"Is everyone on board okay?" Brianna asked. "What about Uncle Bjorn? Where is he?"

"Bjorn is okay. He wasn't badly hurt, just lost his footing for a second." Henry weaved his fingers through his damp hair, brushing it off his forehead. "He is with the men down below. Evidently, a couple of the men in the fish room were knocked about when we took the hit. I think a member of your party is hurt as well. The captain has alerted the coast guard. They are on their way. We're heading back to port and have arranged to meet them before we reach shore."

"How serious are the injuries?" Conner demanded.

"We think a few broken bones, a head wound, maybe."

Brianna gasped, then headed toward the stairs leading below deck. "Who was hurt? Who from our team?"

"Wait." Conner grasped her hand. "I'm sure they're being taken care of. You'll only get in the way."

"What about my uncle? I need to check on him."

"He is okay," Henry assured her. "But I think the Russian gentleman from your team is injured."

"Then we better go check." Conner pulled on her hand, and together they descended the staircase.

What she saw when they reached the bottom deck left little to the imagination. Furniture and various equipment were strewn across the entire area. Water from the fish tanks had splashed up over the top and flooded the floor. Several fish splashed about in the puddles. No wonder the men had slipped and fallen. The strength of the collision had been powerful enough to dislodge not only the men but several of the heavier pieces of fishing equipment.

"It had to be a beast of a small boat to cause this much damage," Conner stated, turning to Lars who was talking to one of the crew, rubbing his forehead. "Are you hurt?"

"No. I'm fine, just a bit shaken," Lars said. "But Ivan is injured. He hit his head hard and passed out. I think there are broken ribs as well. A couple of the crew members removed a door and placed him on it to take him to the crew's quarters to rest until help arrives."

Brianna spotted her uncle leaning over one of his men and went to his side.

"Are you really okay, Uncle?" She put her hand on his shoulder.

He turned and faced her. His grim expression highlighted the fact that he was dismayed over the incident, more than hurt. With good reason. "I am fine," he assured her. "You should go change, settle in my cabin, and relax until we get back to port. We can manage here."

"I'm fine and an extra hand if you need it. Both

Conner and I are okay, a little shaken up as well after our tumble, but we weren't hurt." With their day's mission aborted, Brianna was only too willing to keep her mind busy elsewhere, instead of sitting around waiting and fretting about Conner's spoken thoughts over this incident being too much of a coincidence to let it go unchecked. Apparently, Conner was beginning to consider Bob's innuendoes as well. Was someone out to disrupt their mission on purpose? Was Sven Olson involved? And why them?

"What happened to the boat that hit us?" Conner asked. "Was it damaged? Did any of the crew make contact with them? Question them? Where is it?"

Silence filled the space around them. Brianna scanned the group that suddenly seemed tongue-tied.

"They must not have realized what they did to our ship or were too shocked that it happened," one of the crew members recounted. "We lost sight of them in this heavy fog. It happened so fast. They turned their vessel around and hightailed it up along the coast. They were probably out for a good time and more than likely drunk."

Who would be drunk this early in the morning? Brianna wanted to ask but refrained.

"Did anyone get a good look at the boat before it disappeared? Did they recognize it?" Conner continued to question the men standing around, looking confused. Again, silence. Again, he shook his head, gave her a resigned look, and then motioned for her and Lars to follow him toward the staircase. Uncle Bjorn followed.

"We should report this to the head of the Arctic Project." Brianna wanted this second...no, third...incident to go on record.

"Are you aware of the car incident that Brie and I were involved in last week?" Conner asked Bjorn. "Your niece was injured and is still recovering from her bruised shoulder and head injury."

"No. What accident? Brianna, were you hurt? Why didn't you say so last night? My dear, your aunt will be upset you didn't confide in her. Does Kristina know?"

"No. But then it was only a slight mishap, and I'm doing fine. Nothing is broken, Uncle."

"Still, why do you think that has anything to do with today's mishap?" Bjorn asked the group at large.

"I know where you are going with this, Conner," Lars interjected. "But I don't think today's mishap is connected. I'm sure the heavy fog has something to do with it."

"Then why didn't they stick around to see if we were okay?" Conner turned and pointed his finger at Bjorn. "Which begs the question—was your ship seriously damaged? Or just Ivan and your crew members?"

Brianna scrunched her eyebrows in concern as she faced her uncle, also anticipating his answer.

"Our ship is slightly damaged. Shaken, more like. But minor repairs are being taken care of as we speak. Nothing serious."

"But others aren't so lucky," Brie spoke up. "I'm beginning to think along the same lines as Bob Wilkins—and Conner. Someone is out to sabotage our mission. But who? How many more people have to be injured before we wake up and start investigating these 'minor' incidents before someone gets killed?"

"Are you suggesting we actually take Bob's innuendos seriously?" Lars suggested. "Check deeper into Sven Olson's background?"

"Sven Olson?" Bjorn's astonished tone at the man's name had everyone looking his way, waiting for him to continue. "He has been very helpful in our operations and is a frequent visitor. He works for the Norwegian Fishing Federation. I hear he is also one of the members on the other team. I'm surprised you even consider him suspect of whatever crime you're suggesting."

"Yes, but according to Bob, who is also on the other team, there is a slight possibility that Olson was involved in a black-market operation back in Lobster Cove, Maine." Conner scanned those gathered around, who were busy putting things back in place but had suddenly stopped to listen to their conversation. "From what I gather, he disappeared just prior to the ring being apprehended."

Once again silence followed. Brianna watched her uncle for any signs of concern. She held her breath, waiting to see what his response would be, but her uncle turned from the group when she heard the loud horn from the coast guard's boat as they approached. Within minutes the coast guard were on board tending to Ivan and the injured crew members, readying them for transport to the hospital.

"I'm going with Ivan," Lars stated. He accompanied her uncle and the others as they maneuvered the stretchers up the steep, narrow stairs. "I'll see you back at the hotel."

As much as she wanted to follow them, she hesitated. Her uncle was okay. She'd only be in the way. Still, she felt compelled to be on hand if anything else went wrong. About to say the heck with it and follow the others, she felt a firm hand on her upper arm hold her in place. She swung around to find Conner watching her, eyebrows raised.

"It will do no good to hamper their efforts to get them off the ship. Besides, at this point, I suspect we will be safer on board."

"Do you think this was an accident? Or that it was intended for us?"

He shook his head. His pinched lips caused dimples to form in both cheeks. "I honestly don't know. But better safe than sorry."

She hated that term. But he was right. Resigned, she took a deep breath and focused on his shadowed, concerned eyes. "What do you suggest we do now?"

"We need to talk." Conner's low tones whispered for her ears only. "Preferably in private where we won't be interrupted. Let's go to your uncle's quarters after we change out of these wet suits. I think it's time we both shared what we are really looking for on this expedition."

Maybe he was right. Maybe it was about time she shared her concerns with someone else on the team. Someone she could trust. After all they'd been through so far, Conner was nothing but trustworthy when it came to her well-being.

She nodded her agreement. His hand slid down her arm, and he slipped her hand in his. It felt warm, comforting, and safe. She was disappointed when he let go and they went their respective ways to change into dry clothes.

"I'll meet you back at your uncle's cabin."

She made her way to the locker where she had stored her clothes. A changing room was two doors down, and she was relieved to shut the door behind her. She leaned against it and took in a steadying breath. She wasn't looking forward to this particular private conversation with Conner Holt.

Chapter Eight

Conner stood by the window looking out over the fogged-in ocean, his arms folded across his chest, when Brianna opened the door to her uncle's quarters.

"What are you looking for? Or should I say, what are you able to see in all that swirling mist?" She tried to lighten the tenseness in the room.

"Looking for answers to whatever the hell is going on." He swung around, and by the look on his face, she hadn't achieved the result she had hoped for. "If I didn't know any better, I'd swear someone is out to get us. Or one of us."

"Wait. One of us?" she exclaimed. "You mean they—whoever they are—might be out to get me!" She shouldn't be so surprised, with the close connection to the family and the innuendoes Bob had been throwing around about her family and their connection to Sven since arriving in Tromsø. She pulled out a chair next to the table, sat, and folded her hands on the glass-covered wooden surface to keep them from shaking.

Stay vigilant.

"What makes you think this wasn't an accident?" she asked, focusing on his eyes, not sure what she was looking for, only to see questionable accusation staring back at her.

"You're kidding, right?" he asked. "This is the third time we've been involved in an *incident* that almost cost us our lives." Conner joined her at the table. "So tell me. What do you know about a black-market op that's funneling from here to the Italian markets?"

"What? What are you talking about?" She sat up straight. Why was he questioning *her* about a black-market op? What did she know about that? Nothing. Bob would be the one to answer those questions, not her. She knew little but had been warned to keep an eye out for…what? Helen hadn't been specific. What was she holding back?

"So your job here with Wild and Wonderful is legit?" he queried. "You aren't on assignment to uncover a profiteering ring that started in the States? Or to help cover up operations from your family's fishing business?"

Brianna pushed back from the table and stood; the chair fell backward onto the low-pile carpet. Conner sat as still as a statue, watching her, not batting an eye. Affronted by his accusations, she wanted to walk out, but they were still on her uncle's boat and still at sea. There was nowhere to go. Besides, she had a few questions of her own for Mr. Conner Holt. She walked around the table, stared down at him, and confronted him, her hands crossed in front of her heaving chest.

"So tell me, Mr. Holt, as a climatologist on this expedition, what is it you're really up to? Seems to me you've been keeping a sharp eye on everyone since you arrived. Including me. So is *your* purpose for being here legit? Or are you only on board to keep an eye on the climate?"

"Touché. Let's just say there is a lot more to being a climatologist than weather-watching."

"Just so you know, I'm not hiding a damn thing,"

she ground out, holding her head high. "I'm here solely to check out the aquifer, the fish, and their natural habitat, as well as what happens to them after they are either transferred to a fishing operation or having been raised there. If someone is after *me*, I have no idea who or why."

Hands on hips now, she circled back around the table, picked her chair up, and positioned it under the table, then sat. "Look, Conner, there may be a few who suspect my uncle's fish farm is involved in something nefarious. Like not keeping an accurate count and reporting it. After all, it's one of the bigger fishing operations here in Tromsø. But I honestly don't believe they are, or would be, involved in a black-market scheme. Their business has always been solvent, even though their catch has been a bit lower than usual. According to my cousin, it's nothing compared to other operations up along the coastline. There has been a sighting of a potential virus in several of the fish in case you aren't aware." She raised her eyebrows, questioning his knowledge. She didn't believe for one moment that he wasn't aware of potential viruses. "If I'd been able to dive today, I would have checked it out to determine if that's the case."

He returned her questioning stare. She waited for the other shoe to drop. What knowledge did he think she had that would have someone target them? Try to scare them away? From what? Or worst-case scenario, kill them? Why?

"Perhaps we should arrange another dive later this afternoon so you can check it out."

"I think we need to check in on Ivan and my uncle's crew members first, to see how they are doing. And, hopefully, find out what happened. Perhaps, if you don't have any information to contribute to this conversation, the coast guard and others on this ship might."

"I don't have information at this time. Otherwise, I wouldn't be asking you what you know."

"Great. So remind me again why someone might be after you, the climatologist. How could you, being on this research team, be such a threat to…what? More rain. Lots of sunshine melting the ice?"

Across the table, he seemed to be carefully searching for words he thought she might want to hear. Was he being cagy on purpose? What did he think she was hiding?

She suspected there was a lot more to Conner Holt than met the eye.

Before he could respond, the door opened and her uncle strode in and approached the table.

"Are you two okay?" He sat at the head of the table in his captain's chair, leaned his arms on the table, and swiveled his head back and forth between the two of them.

"Yes, I'm fine, Uncle. It was quite a shock but nothing compared to what Ivan and your men experienced and are going through."

"And you, Mr. Holt? How are you doing?"

"I'm fine, also. Do you have any more information on what transpired?"

"Simply a case of hit and run, as you Americans say. But the authorities will be looking into it. I'm sure it's nothing more than a group of boys out for an adventure who ended up not seeing where they were going in this heavy fog."

"Still, after what we've been through before arriving

in Tromsø, I'm sure you can understand why we're concerned it was something more than an adventure gone bad."

The look on Conner's face confirmed her own gut reflexes. Neither of them believed her uncle. Suddenly, she was wondering if her uncle *was* covering for someone and was really a part of a black-market scheme. But who was he covering for? Was it someone on one of the research teams? Could it be Sven Olson?

The door opened behind her. Her uncle's crew member, Franklin, strode to the table with the announcement that they were ready to dock.

"I have vehicles ready to take you to the hospital to check on the injured. I understand the authorities are waiting to interview everyone involved and assess what took place. Should I tell Henry to handle them?"

"Yes. And thanks," her uncle responded. "I'll meet you on the dock in ten minutes."

Her uncle stood, waited until Franklin left the room, and then walked to the windows overlooking the ocean. He stood gazing at the fog starting to lift as silence filled the room. A moment later, he turned and faced them. She didn't like what she saw etched on his face. Gone was the happy-go-lucky man she knew her uncle to be. Pensive, pinched lips and piercing dark eyes told a different story. His next words almost broke her heart.

"I have a feeling you both think there is more to this accident. And that I, or my company, have something to do with it."

"Trying to destroy your own vessel leads me to believe that's not the case," Conner stated. "Someone on the inside that you aren't aware of might be an alternative to consider."

Carol Henry

"Or someone you've worked closely with over the past," Brianna interjected, glad to see her uncle's facial expression relax. "If you have any information that you can think of that might give us a clue, it could shed light on what's been happening to Conner and me."

"This is the first time I'm hearing that my business might be involved in anything shady," her uncle said, hands flat on the table as he leaned forward. "You seem to know more than I do. Is that really why you are here inspecting my operation? Is there something you're not telling me? Something I should know?"

"I honestly don't know what's going on, Uncle Bjorn. At this point, like Conner just mentioned, I don't think you would be involved. I can't believe you would purposely have someone ram into your main vessel and cause such casualties. I know you wouldn't intentionally hurt anyone."

"Brie is right." Conner stood and laid his hand on her uncle's shoulder. "Let's wait and see what the authorities come up with, and we can go from there."

"Thanks." Her uncle nodded as he placed his hands in his pockets.

"In the meantime, I'd like to arrange another dive to check out the possibility of a virus," Brianna suggested. "I was hoping you could arrange for a smaller craft to take us out early in the morning." She stood as well, hoping that her request would break the tension in the room. "We're here for another day before we move on up to the North Cape."

Her uncle didn't hesitate. "I'll have Henry make arrangements for seven thirty tomorrow morning. Will that work for you?"

"Perfect. Thanks, Uncle Bjorn."

"Your aunt is expecting you for dinner again tonight. Conner, you are invited as well."

After the tense conversation they had just had, before and after her uncle joined them, she wasn't sure having Conner accompany her to dinner was a good idea. Or why her uncle had invited him.

What was her uncle thinking?

****

The wharf buzzed with the news of the mishap when they disembarked from the fishing craft. The heavy mist had lifted, and the sun peeked through, giving a mystical aura to the surrounding harbor. Conner, Brianna, and her uncle were escorted to a waiting taxi and driven to the hospital.

Upon arrival, they met members from the other team, along with family members of the crew that had heard about the mishap. The waiting room was large with round tables, chairs, and a series of windows that overlooked the harbor. Meant to provide a relaxing atmosphere, the packed room was anything but serene today.

Shocked to see members from the other team, Brianna shook her head as she spotted Sven holding center court with two newsmen, even though he hadn't been on her uncle's boat. They paused to take in the scene. Turning to observe Conner's reaction, she wasn't disappointed. He gave her a slight nod, and together they headed toward the others. Lars immediately made his way over to Sondra, who was engaged in conversation with Bob and Stefan. No sooner had Lars reached Sondra's side, interrupting her, than she turned her head and scanned the area. Sondra's facial expression instantly turned from concern to her normal flirtatiousness as soon as she saw Conner. But before Sondra could disengage from the others, Conner latched on to Brianna's arm and drew her toward several health professionals shaking their heads at the chaos surrounding them.

Glad for the distraction, Brianna let Conner lead her away, and together they silently approached the hospital staff. Not surprisingly, the staff wasn't able to divulge medical information on the men's conditions. Instead, they gave them the usual assurances that the men were being well taken care of, and they would go through proper channels to release information when it became available.

Averse to interrupting Sondra's group discussion with Lars, despite wanting to know what was going on with them and how they had heard about the incident so soon, Brianna nudged her way through the crowd to an empty chair in the far corner of the room. Conner followed.

"I think we're going to be here a while."

His impatient and tired voice led her to believe he was just as weary of the whole project as she had become.

"How about we go to the cafeteria and get a coffee? I could use something stronger, but I don't believe they serve anything stronger than caffeine in this establishment."

She had to agree. Sitting around wouldn't solve anything. Lars would be sure to fill them in later. She hadn't spotted her uncle but was confident he would be around somewhere, checking on his men.

"Let's go." She was surprised he didn't want to stay and find out what Sondra and her team were discussing.

Hopefully, Lars would fill them in later.

As they left the room, Sven had obviously finished with the newsmen and was now standing farther down the corridor. He leaned one arm against the wall, the other pointing at two burley-looking, heavily bearded men. Their voices were guarded; she wasn't able to hear what they were saying. Obviously, Sven wasn't happy with them, nor they with Sven.

"Come on, let's go this way." Conner tugged her arm, and together they turned and headed in the opposite direction. Brianna crossed her fingers, hoping Sven hadn't seen them.

When they reached the cafeteria, they ordered a coffee and made their way past several cafeteria-style tables to one at the end of the room near the window.

"I feel I owe you an apology for the way I acted back on the ship." Conner sat across from her, opened two packets of sugar, and stirred them into his coffee, which was already loaded with cream.

Brianna followed suit, took a deep sip, sat back in her chair, and placed her cup on the table, her hands wrapped around the Styrofoam container. "So what aren't you telling me, Holt?"

"What makes you think I'm keeping something from you?"

"You appear to be more interested in wrongdoing than in climate change lately."

"Can't I be interested in both?" He sipped from his coffee before he continued, looking deep into her eyes.

For the life of her, she was having a hard time reading him. His eyes, bright from the sun shining through the window, were more mesmerizing than concerning. Still, she felt there was something he wasn't telling her. Something she was missing? But what?

"Let's just say that I'm as concerned as you are over the mishaps we've been experiencing. Bob's innuendoes have started to raise red flags that even you have to consider are legit. How it might tie into your uncle's fishing operation is anyone's guess."

"And what's your guess? How do you think it ties in with my uncle's business?" She sat back, waiting, hoping he could give her a clue as to what they should be focusing on.

"After today, I have no idea. Perhaps they were trying to throw our research progress off? For whatever reason."

Brianna thought for a moment, sipped her coffee, and gazed out the window at the harbor. Fishing ships, passenger ships, and speedboats were lined up along the dock while tourists meandered around the streets. Her mind whirled. Why would someone want to impede their research?

Before she could ask Conner for his opinion, Lars was heading their way, coffee in hand. Maybe now they would get some answers.

"May I join you?" Lars sat, not waiting for an answer. "I just got word that Ivan is going to be in the hospital for a few more days. He's off the team due to his injuries."

"How serious are they?" Conner asked.

"What about my uncle's men? How are they doing?"

"They don't think Ivan's injuries are life-threatening. But one of your uncle's men is also going to have an extended stay in the hospital. The other one will be discharged tomorrow with minor injuries."

"Any word on what actually happened?" Conner asked, pushing his coffee aside and leaning against the table.

"Not definite. I called Mr. Erickson. He asked me to arrange a meeting with both teams for tomorrow. He's asked the other team to stay put another day before they head up north. He plans to attend the meeting. I hope you have nothing else on the agenda."

"Other than this afternoon meeting to inspect my uncle's inoculation processing facility, we've arranged another dive tomorrow morning," Brianna informed Lars. "I'm hoping to make up for not being able to dive today. But we should be free to attend a meeting with Mr. Erickson in the afternoon."

"Good plan. Mind if I join you for the dive?"

"Not at all."

"Good. Hopefully, being down one member of our team isn't going to affect our research efforts."

Brianna had to agree with Lars. Especially as it was Ivan who was laid up. He would have been an asset the closer they got to the Russian boarder.

Chapter Nine

The Kelseys' ocean farm and inoculation facility, located offshore farther up the coast, was full of activity when Conner, Brianna, and Lars arrived. The sea cage consisted of a rigid steel structure with extensive circular permeable net panels reminiscent of a huge wagon wheel, with the main facility in the center hub. Together they made their way along one of the walkways resembling wheel spokes that jutted out from the main facility. Below and immersed in the ocean were large nets that held the fish in place. Brianna's uncle led them to the main facility where eight large water tanks were situated on either side of a wooden platform that contained fresh seawater. Four men were positioned between two tanks, each retrieving fish from one container, inoculating them, and then tossing them into the holding tank on the other side. In all, the four men were kept busy handling the fish. It was a well-run operation. The men were adept at limiting the amount of time the fish were out of the water.

After observing the operation for half an hour, they were escorted through the facility. Conner didn't see anything amiss or anything that would implicate Brianna's uncle in any wrongdoing. The operation seemed legit and well run.

"As you know, we dry the fish in the open. As you can see over to the left. That process has finished for the season." Bjorn pointed to two empty drying racks that resembled giant dinosaur-size inverted ribs glistening in the late afternoon sun.

"Later, we will rehydrate the dried fish by soaking them in lye and water for processing. But then, I'm sure you are aware of the procedure."

Again, Conner was satisfied with the inspection. He'd taken water temperatures while out along the rim of the sea cage. As they reached shore once again, he longed to take Brie aside so they could finish their earlier conversation before Lars had shown up and interrupted them. He needed to clear the air between them. But right now, there was no time to get her aside from the others before going back to the hotel to prepare to go to the Kelseys' for dinner.

****

Being they were in the land of the midnight sun, the evening remained bright, well into the night. Brianna's samples from the various locations they had visited earlier had been sent off to the federation's testing lab for evaluation. The results wouldn't be available for a couple of days, but Mr. Erickson would be the one to record them, along with all the other data the two teams had been collecting. She would send tomorrow's samples separately, in order to keep them designated by location. But tonight she was ready to relax. As much as she could with Conner meeting the rest of her family.

Arriving at Uncle Bjorn and Aunt Anna's later that evening, with the bright midnight sun overhead, felt as if they were arriving in the afternoon. She felt as if she had already lived two days in one; her energy level had dropped. The doctor had cautioned her to look for signs of a concussion such as dizziness, excessive tiredness, or vomiting. Thankfully, she hadn't had any of those symptoms. Her headaches were tapering off, but she wanted to keep on top of them before they got worse. And with the stress of this morning's incident, it was time for another pain pill.

Brianna and Conner were met with open arms when they arrived at the Kelsey homestead. Once again, Aunt Anna hugged her and whispered words of comfort over her parents' illness, while her cousin Kristina jumped in and insisted she be introduced to Conner.

"So, Conner, this is my cousin, Kristina Kelsey. Kristina, Conner. He's the climatologist on our project."

She didn't blame Kris for her flamboyant welcome. Conner was one handsome gentleman and had been a comforting and caring companion to her during and after the incidents, despite their last confrontation. For a time, she thought something might be developing between them. Dare she hope? Yes, Sondra found him attractive enough to all but trip over her own feet to get to know Conner, but he hadn't seemed interested. Was he only being considerate to her because they were on the same team? Because he had asked her to join him on his foray into the fjords and felt responsible for the accidents and her well-being?

"Pleased to meet you." Kristina extended her hand in greeting. "I've heard so much about you from Brianna. I'm sorry to hear about your mishaps."

"Mishaps?" Aunt Anna wailed, her hands quickly mounted on her hips, her eyes popping wide as she directed them at Brianna. "What mishaps? Are you okay? What happened?"

"Now, Anna"—Uncle Bjorn shook his head—"I mentioned the mishap this morning and that Brianna is okay. Remember? It is one of their team members that was injured."

"I'm fine. Really, Aunt Anna. No need to be upset. I'm in good hands."

Brianna watched Kristina's smile grow at the comment. The implication of being in good hands obviously had Kristina thinking there was something going on between her and Conner. But even though Brianna was becoming more than fond of Conner, she knew nothing could come of her infatuation with him.

"Please, come sit down. Dinner is ready." Her aunt let out her breath she'd been holding and motioned them toward the kitchen table. "I hope you like cod."

Everyone laughed as they sat around the table. Not liking cod in Norway was unthinkable, especially as owners of a fishing business had to deal with cod on a daily basis. After a hearty meal and light, general conversation, they gathered in the family sitting room. Conner sat next to her on the small sofa, while the others sat in easy chairs on the other side of a round coffee table. All it took was for Kristina to mention the implication of the family operation being in question for the conversation to take a turn in the wrong direction. Again. Brianna sighed and watched as her uncle shook his head. His expression conflicted at the implication that his operation was thought to be involved in a black-market scheme.

"Maybe you should take a closer look at your catch figures," Brianna suggested. "From what we've learned, others are having similar problems."

"It's just a matter of cross-checking to make sure everything is in order," Conner added, sitting forward, his arms resting on his knees. "It's not an accusation, Mr.

Kelsey, but a precautionary measure Brianna's suggesting."

Kristina crossed her arms as she looked at Brianna, then Conner with raised eyebrows before focusing on her father. "Why? We don't have a problem like the others up along the coast, do we, *Far*?"

"I've discussed this with my men," her uncle said. "Henry hasn't seen anything out of the ordinary. But just so we are clear on what's afoot, let's get this out in the open, once and for all."

"Thank you, Mr. Kelsey." Conner kept an even tone and sat back.

Brianna felt his shoulder brush against hers. She'd been held against his shoulder after the accidents and felt the comforting connection. Now it was different. He seemed tense, although he personified an open and relaxed demeanor. She knew the situation he was about to impart wasn't something to disregard or the family wanted to hear, but it finally needed to be said. She was thankful Conner was the one that was going to tell them what was going on, which would leave her off the hook for informing on her family.

"I can't stress enough that these three incidents, including the one this morning, aren't coincidental. All three were targeted at our team, specifically Brianna and myself. Although your niece wasn't injured in this incident, she did suffer injuries in the previous ones."

"But there is no evidence to connect those incidents," Kristina stated. "I've heard talk in town, and word is those kids have been identified and corroborated that they lost control of their boat and couldn't pull back fast enough before they rammed into *Far's* boat."

Silence filled the small, cozy room. Brianna waited.

She could tell Conner wasn't about to argue with them, so she remained silent. She didn't want to get into a rift with her family and cause trouble until they knew for certain if they were involved. Why, oh why, had Kristina brought the topic up tonight?

Conner finally broke the silence. "From the start, there has been innuendoes circulating as to a black-market scheme up along the coast and that several of the fishing companies are involved. Yours was one of them."

"As I said before, I'm aware of the talk. But who has implicated me? Where did this information come from?" her uncle asked calmly but with a twitch to his eye.

"I can't divulge that information until the project is completed." Conner sat forward again, as if to make a point. "But there have been a couple of the members who had tie-ins with a black-market ring back in the US with connections to Norway. Sven Olson, to be exact."

"But he works with the federation." Uncle Bjorn sounded shocked.

Kristina's eyes went wide. She sat forward and glared at Conner. Aunt Anna sat quietly, taking it all in.

"Yes. And he's on the other team, as you are aware," Conner confirmed the obvious.

"And has helped us out several times," Kristina stated, the astonished look on her face priceless. "I don't believe it. He can't be involved. What makes them think it's him?"

Good question. Other than listening to Bob and his theories, Brianna had no solid evidence against Sven. If Conner did, he hadn't shared that information with her. Yet.

Brianna couldn't hold back any longer. "I'm hoping our dive tomorrow will help corroborate or put a stop to their theory, one way or another. If climate change is causing a disruption in the aquifer, we'll be able to check it out with more samples closer to the sea bottom—plants and other marine life."

She caught Conner's slight grin at her starting to side with him in regard to climate change. His reaction warmed her insides.

"Excellent," her uncle confirmed. "We will take a smaller boat out for the dive. I'll meet you on the dock at seven."

****

"That was a smart move on your part, my friend," Sven congratulated Gianni over his cell phone. "Way to make it look like a bunch of teenagers having fun and rammed into the fishing vessel by mistake. A great decoy to shake them off our tail. Unfortunately, one of their team members was hurt and is hospitalized. He's off the team for the duration."

"You give me too much credit," Gianni crowed. "My men orchestrated the drill and almost killed themselves to save our asses. Blaming it on drunken youngsters covered their own asses."

"Whatever it took to get it done. However, they made it look as if Team Two is obviously being targeted, which makes Team One look rather suspect. We need to rectify the situation. We need to find a way to alleviate that situation. Something minor to make it look like Team Two isn't the only team being affected. I talked to your man at the hospital. The one who drove the boat. He shouldn't have shown up there. Too risky."

"He did his job. You shouldn't have approached him. Perhaps we shouldn't plan any further incidents to try to stop the investigations? Perhaps you are being too

124

paranoid and we should just go about our business and let everyone do their research as scheduled. We can work around it."

Sven couldn't believe what Gianni was suggesting. Damn it. They were getting closer to finalizing their catch quota through the area for the Asian markets. He had to be careful to keep his cover through the federation intact. But how else could he stop the project from going forward?

"My team was supposed to head up the coast to the North Cape tomorrow. Because of this accident, we're being detained by the director of the project. He's scheduled a meeting to discuss the incidents. I need to be there to deflect our involvement. After we leave Tromsø, we both have other fisheries to inspect. The other team won't be following us immediately. I suggest you come up with a minor incident of some sort to befall our team before we get to the cape. Get your men on it, ASAP."

****

Mountains in the distance rose up to meet the morning sun. The day promised to be another bright cloudless day in paradise. Brianna took in a deep breath; the brisk Arctic air filled her lungs as she walked along the dock toward her uncle's large motorboat. Lars and Conner followed behind, deep in conversation. A slight wind brushed against her cheeks. She couldn't be more excited about this morning's adventure, never having experienced an Arctic dive this deep before. She couldn't help but wonder what exciting sights she was about to discover along the Arctic Sea floor. Hopefully, it would be something, anything, to substantiate her hopes of discovery she'd discussed the night before. Despite the importance of the work she had been doing for this research project, she had become more excited about the adventure itself than the research it entailed.

Her uncle's boat was fully equipped to handle everyone and their equipment. Once everyone was onboard, it was only a matter of minutes before Henry set sail. They motored toward the northern end of the fjord. By the time he dropped anchor at their designated location, they were dressed in their warmer orange diving suits and ready to finish preparing for their dive. Despite the frigid ocean temperatures, they anticipated only spending no more than a half hour investigating the deep ocean's floor.

Brianna joined Conner and Lars as they put on their full face masks and fins. Next came their oxygen tanks. Brianna strapped a looped belt around her waist for storing samples.

"Are you ready to do this?" Conner grinned, obviously as eager as she was to take the plunge. He tugged on her hand and drew her closer to the side of the boat. His firm grip sent a warm tingle up her arm that circled her entire body. The sensation left her speechless. She could only nod her agreement. And hoped another boat didn't come careening into them like before.

Lars stepped beside Conner, and before she had a chance to delve into her reaction to Conner's sizzling touch, Lars stepped in between them and nudged them closer to the edge of the boat. Without further words from either man, she found herself hand in hand with Conner, being nudged over the side of the boat, slipping into the deep blue Arctic's frigid waters before she had a chance to brace herself for the shock of the change in temperature to her body's system. Adjusting her eyes to the underwater visibility took a few seconds. She focused on Conner, who appeared to seamlessly be in tune to his surroundings. Of course, he was familiar with the colder climates. Her, not so much. It was exhilarating. Her insides warmed despite the frigid temperatures. But she was ready to delve into the deep.

Taking a minute to view the area before they started their deeper dive, she knew it would become darker as they approached the sea floor, but for now the sun shone down through the clear chilly waters, and it was a sight to behold. Conner swam alongside her while Lars pushed on ahead. Lars switched on his high-powered light as they dove deeper, enabling them to see what was in front of them. Suddenly, out of nowhere, a pair of orcas swam right at them, then quickly jutted up in front of them, obviously startled by the light's beam, catching Brianna off guard. She'd come in contact with other smaller marine life before but never an orca. The orca immediately veered to the left and shot overhead, missing them, stirring the ocean, making waves before swimming out of sight. Conner grabbed her hand to steady her, then pointed to the left where a pod of wolf fish whooshed past them. Brianna's insides warmed again, the unexpected sighting a great start to her underworld adventure.

Over the course of the next half hour, Brianna was delighted as they encountered an assortment of marine life—cod, scallops, stingray, haddock, and even a smattering of halibut. As they reached the sea floor, innumerable species resembled an underwater jungle of kelp and various shades and species of coral, while sea anemones swayed as they swam past the various plant life. Brianna didn't hesitate to retrieve samples of everything. She placed them in individual containers connected to the belt circling her waist. She couldn't wait to have them evaluated. They appeared healthy and well-developed.

Conner, having been busy checking and double-checking the water temperature at different levels, suddenly nudged her, then pointed to several large king crabs clawing in the sediment, making more of a cloudy aura in their wake. Lars, who was busy taking pictures, quickly grabbed one of the king crabs and held it up for inspection, claws dangling in front of him in protest. He swung to the side, pushed it out from him to release it, and took a quick picture. Then he pointed upward, indicating it was time to return to the boat.

Loathe to leave the incredible underworld adventure, Brianna joined the others, and together they resurfaced and climbed back on board.

Beaming, she was ready to do a happy dance, although she would have liked to spend more time below. Their morning adventure couldn't have been more awesome, exceeding her expectations. Given that Conner had remained by her side the entire time, pointing out significant sights she might have otherwise missed, she had a hard time not wrapping her arms around him and giving him a hug. He stepped toward her, a wide smile on his handsome face. Did he want to hug her, too? An indication that he enjoyed the experience as well? Perhaps her thoughts were obvious, and he was going to grant her wish. However, Lars intervened, once again, as he cut in between them in order to lay his equipment on the bench behind them.

"Yes, an awesome adventure." Lars smiled from ear to ear. He proceeded to take off his facial gear. "A job well done. Did you see that large king crab? Wow! What a beauty. Doesn't look like the water temperature, or anything else, has hampered their domain."

"I knew you would enjoy diving in this location." Brianna's uncle joined them. "Did you find what you were looking for?"

"I did catch a slight bit of warming as we went deeper." Conner continued to remove his diving equipment. "But that's not significant. It's the temperature in between that has me concerned."

Henry stepped forward and helped Brianna with her tank and gear. She secured the various samples she'd taken and placed them in the dry case Henry had waiting for her.

"I didn't see anything amiss down below, at first glance. All the samples I took appear in prime condition. However, lab results will confirm if in fact I'm correct. Thanks so much for taking us back out today, Uncle Bjorn."

"Glad you were able to have a chance to unwind and enjoy yourself after all you've been through."

She was ready to decompress and prepare for their journey toward Honningsvåg and the North Cape. And try to keep her mind on the job at hand. And not on Conner Holt.

"Will we have time to stop and visit the North Cape site when we get to Honningsvåg?" Brianna couldn't help but ask. She'd been longing to experience the adventure of standing on Europe's most northern point, next to the large globe statue.

"As a matter of fact, we're scheduled to check out a couple smaller fishing farms not far from there. Depending on how our meeting goes later today, we can think about taking a break and check it out," Lars said.

"I'd love that," Brianna gushed. "Standing next to the Global Monument Statue, up close, has been on my bucket list for a long time."

"Get ready to cross it off your list." Conner grinned, raised his hand, and pretended to check it off a list he held in the other hand.

"I'm meeting with Sondra this afternoon before our meeting so we can compare team notes," Lars informed them as they exited the boat once it docked back in the harbor. "But first I'm going to the hospital and check in on Ivan. See how he's doing. I'll catch up with you later this evening at our scheduled meeting with Mr. Erickson. We can make arrangements for our departure then."

"It will be interesting to see what they've come up with so far," Conner said. "See if the other team has run into any problems along the way."

Brianna's excitement of the morning dive dwindled. She wasn't looking forward to the meeting with the other team. Too much had already happened, and she wasn't convinced that the two teams were working in tandem toward the same goal.

Chapter Ten

"I'm glad you agreed to have lunch with me. I thought we had an excellent dive this morning." Conner leaned forward and folded his hands on the top of the small patio-style table. He'd chosen a more secluded corner in the hotel's restaurant where he and Brianna could talk without being interrupted or overheard.

"It was awesome. The sea life, including the plants, looked healthy enough. I sent samples out as soon as we got back." She leaned forward as well.

The sparkle in her eyes made his insides smile. Good Lord, she was getting to him more and more each day. He took a deep breath to control his thoughts. "Look, I want to apologize again for coming on rather strong yesterday. Clear the air between us. Find out how you're really doing after our initial mishap. How are the headaches? And your arm? You seem to be coping well."

"I'm doing okay. The light bruising on my right upper arm hasn't bothered me at all. In fact, I've had no pain this last week. As for the headaches, they've dwindled, and I haven't taken any pain meds since last night."

"That's good to know. I was hoping that was the case. I haven't noticed any signs that you were in pain. Wasn't sure if it was the meds helping or not."

"I'm fine. Still trying to wrap my head around everything that has been going on."

"Look, I didn't mean to upset you in any way yesterday."

"You did come on rather strong, as you say. But I understand." She sat back, looked down at the table, then back up at him. "We've all been under a lot of stress and pressure on this expedition. None of which is your fault. Or mine."

Brianna was gracious to be so understanding. It couldn't be easy for her to think her family was involved in any wrongdoing, and for her to be on a team that was investigating them. She had wrapped a protective shell around her in regard to her family, not to mention the accidents they'd been involved in. He hated to admit it, but he had become rather fond of her in such a short time. Of course, he was concerned for her well-being. Still, he had wanted to scoop her up and wrap his arms around her after their splendid dive this morning. Kissing those enticing lips of hers had crossed his mind. It had been an exhilarating experience with her by his side. He also knew that nothing could come of his growing desire whenever he was in her presence. Like now. Relationships and his occupation didn't mesh.

"I have to ask a personal question, Conner. I hope you don't mind. And I hope you'll be honest with me."

Her serious facial expression gave him pause and brought his mind back to the present. A disconnect with the emotions he'd just been undergoing.

"Ask away. I'll do my best to give you a truthful answer." He wanted to be as honest as he could under the circumstances, no matter her question. He wanted her to trust him.

"What did you mean when you said there was a lot more to being a climatologist than weather-watching?

What exactly are you doing here?"

Damn! Talk about being put on the spot. Her penetrating eyes had him sitting back in his chair. He had to lighten the tension coming from across the table while he tried to quickly determine how much information to divulge.

"Just for the record, that's two questions." It wasn't the question he had anticipated her asking. He lifted his water glass and sipped from it, hiding his astonishment.

"I'm sure your response to either question will amount to the same answer." Her penetrating glare made him nervous. The sparkle in her eyes faded dramatically. Her shoulders pulled up as she sat back in her seat. She was literally putting him on the line. This wasn't the same Brianna from the Arctic dive this morning.

"You'll have to swear on a stack of bibles that you won't divulge what I'm about to tell you."

His attempt to lighten the tense air between them failed. Her expression told him she wasn't at all amused with his glib tone.

"Is it that bad, Conner? Should I be afraid to be seen with you? Is my life in jeopardy when I'm in your company?"

"You are full of questions, aren't you?" His attempt at humor had fallen flatter than a Norwegian pancake.

She continued to sit silently, waiting for him to get serious, her eyes never leaving his. *Shit.* She deserved to know what was going on. She'd been involved in every one of the accidents that had taken place since this project got underway. He was amazed that the dive had gone without incident. Amazed and thankful.

"I'm working undercover." He gave in. "I can't divulge for whom, but needless to say, I'd prefer you promise to keep this to yourself." He saw the shock in her deep-blue eyes and almost wished he'd kept his mouth shut. She could trust him, but could he trust her?

"Promise." She raised her right hand, gave him the Girl Scout Promise sign, and then swiped her fingers over her heart.

His pulse kicked up at her actions and that sexy smile that lit up her face. He hoped he wasn't making a huge mistake by confiding in her. Before he could stop himself, he dove right back in.

"To begin with, Bob Wilkins is correct to a point." He paused, waiting for her reaction to the news to sink in.

"Go on," she prodded, obviously waiting for him to spill the rest of the facts. She leaned forward and rested her elbows on the table and her chin in her folded hands. Then focused on him—eye to eye.

He inhaled, then let it out slowly before he divulged the rest of the news. "They suspect an insider on one of the teams. Bob has his eyes on Sven Olson being the ring leader of an operation funneling mostly cod from here in Norway to Italy's black markets, then on to the Asian markets. However, we're searching for possible connections and have a number of people identified. We need definite proof before we can crack the case. If it's any consolation, we don't think whoever is behind our accidents is targeting you in particular. Your only connection is through Wild and Wonderful, thus Bob, and of course your uncle's fishing operation." Conner let out a deep breath, again waiting for her to grasp the full significance of the situation. Her reaction to the implications of what he had just shared didn't really surprise him.

"What about my uncle's connection? Who fingered him as one of those working with the profiteers?"

"I'm not at liberty to say at this point."

"How worried should I be? My family?"

"Listen, if they wanted to 'take you out,' you wouldn't be sitting here with me right now." He reached across the table and took her hands in his. They were cold. He wanted to warm them, take her in his arms, and comfort her and leave the restaurant and find a more secluded place to continue this conversation. And more.

"I appreciate you confiding in me." She squeezed his hands. "But I've got to say it doesn't make me feel any safer. In fact, it makes me feel less safe."

"Trust me, Brie, I'm looking out for your safety. In fact, Lars has asked me to stick close to you, especially here in Tromsø. From here on out, you don't go anywhere without me."

"So Lars is aware of the situation, too? How many others know? Does Ivan?"

"We aren't sure about Ivan. Lars says he doesn't seem to be improving. He is no longer on the team, as he'll be in the hospital a few more days, then sent home to recover. Any threat that might have come from him, if any, is moot at this point."

"And you don't think that isn't enough to be worried about someone wanting to take me out?" Her eyes grew wide with concern. Her hands grew tighter in his. "Should I quit the team and go back home, now, before something else happens to me? And what about Uncle Bjorn? Is he safe? Is his family safe?"

"After the mishap yesterday, there are tighter securities in place. And yes, you're safe here and in your hotel room. We have a connecting door, if you haven't already noticed. If it will make you feel more secure, you can leave the door open tonight. I'll be there in a heartbeat if you need me."

He'd feel even better if he could simply follow her into her room when they returned to the hotel after the meeting later tonight. To keep her safe, of course.

****

Brianna scanned the occupants of the conference room at the Tromsø Hotel. Mr. Erickson had called the emergency meeting to discuss the complications of the boating accident and Ivan's incapacity to continue with the program. Both teams' members were present, except for Ivan, of course. Brianna couldn't help but wonder what each member knew in regard to the situation she and Conner had discussed over lunch.

On a side note, it was interesting to see that Sondra had seemingly turned her attentions to Stefan Dutlov, the Russian member of her team, as the two sat side by side at the end of the table. Their heads were practically locked together with little space between them. The smile on her face was telling, indicating a more than friendlier relationship, as was Stefan's. For once Sondra seemed to be ignoring Conner's presence. Brianna considered her own relationship with Conner, who was sitting next to her. Although they'd had their ups and downs, her feelings for him had grown more than she had anticipated. His attention to detail, caring, and especially his touch when he held her hand, and kissed her forehead with his enticing lips, had ignited sparks within her that were getting harder and harder to ignore. She knew he wasn't interested in a long-term relationship. Even though he was attentive toward her, he only interested in her as a business partner, looking out for her safety. She'd been there, done that, and didn't want to go there again. Having someone putting their work over a relationship with her wasn't happening again. Being dedicated to one's calling was one thing. Letting it dictate her entire life was another. She wanted a relationship that was an honest-to-goodness shared relationship, not one-sided.

"Before we begin, I want to make official that Ivan Alexander will not be continuing with the project, as his injuries are serious and he is still in the hospital," Mr. Erickson stated, bringing Brianna's mind back to focus on the business at hand.

"Now, we need to address the seriousness of yesterday's accident, as well as the mishaps Conner and Brianna have experienced over the course of this expedition. If anyone has thoughts or relevant information concerning these incidents, you need to speak up before we continue with the federation's mission." He gave eye contact to each member seated around the table, eyebrows raised in question, waiting for someone to speak up.

"I thought the authorities said this was a mere accident." Stefan spoke up. "Nothing but teenagers, delinquents, out of control."

Sondra nodded in agreement. "It is too bad people were injured, but it has nothing to do with our research."

"Actually," Mr. Erickson said, "it does. I am aware that there is a black market operating along the coastal waters here in Norway. There are those who would like to see us disband our research."

"So perhaps we should disband," Sven quickly interjected, sitting back in his chair. His features gave nothing away. "If it's going to keep putting us all in danger, that is, not because someone else wants us to."

The entire room remained silent as if they were contemplating his suggestion. Everyone looked at each other, then back at Mr. Erickson, waiting for his comments.

"I see some of you are surprised," Sven commented as he scanned the occupants gathered around the elongated table. "I don't see why."

"He has a point." Sondra spoke up, filling in another quiet pause. "Our team has gathered enough information to hand over to the federation committee in regard to the aquifer and sea life."

"Yes," Sven readily agreed. "Besides, I hear Conner's assessment of evidence of climate change, and the virus both our teams have uncovered in mostly cod, makes it obvious we have plenty of information the federation can work with and make their recommendations with what we have already provided."

Brianna sat quietly, as did Conner, through the entire conversation. After Conner had indicated earlier that Sven might be involved in the black-market scheme, she wasn't surprised that he wanted to suspend the mission. She was relieved when Mr. Erickson finally spoke up.

"As you might have forgotten, I am the federation's liaison and director of this project. And as we have no hard evidence, so far, that such a situation exists, I only mention this so you can keep your eyes open as we continue north to the Barents Sea. The research goes forward. You will make your way to Honningsvåg as planned. I have arranged for security for each team as you advance north."

Several nodded their agreement. Not wanting to be

obvious, Brianna searched Sven's facial expression from the corner of her eyes. He sat stone-faced, looking directly at Mr. Erickson.

Shit! The guy looked guilty as hell! And disappointed that the project was moving forward.

****

Sven wanted to shut Bob up. He was agitating the men working on the long fishing dock at their current assignment in Hammerfest. Questioning the dock workers about a local black-market ring wasn't smart. With any luck, Gianni and his men would already be out of the area's fishing waters, undetected.

"So you're saying there hasn't been any suspect activity in the area?" Bob questioned, hands on hips, feet planted on the well-worn wooden dock.

"Nothing unusual," the shorter of the two Norwegian dockworkers confirmed while the taller of the two scrunched his eyes and shook his head.

"So you haven't a lower take of your usual catch?"

The taller man stepped back and raised his brows. "No more than usual. We have been told the ice waters are warming."

Sven stepped between Bob and the two men. "And so it has." He needed to intervene before Sondra or Stefan had a chance to join in Bob's interrogation as well. Why had the federation put Bob on his team? The man was an interfering, infuriating drain on his watch and was up to proving there was a black-market operation in the works. *Damn!*

As he was about to apologize to the two men, a sudden ruckus erupted behind him. He turned to see what had caused the commotion, only to be caught up short as he recognized Gianni's goons. They were barreling toward him, hands flying in the air as if the world were coming to an end, one chasing the other. Without stopping or circling around them, the first man knocked into Bob, tripping him to the side, causing him to land on his backside. Sven and Stefan rushed to help Bob. But before Sven could reach Bob, he found himself being shoved over the side of the dock by the second man. He hit his head on the dock post, spun sideways, and tumbled into the harbor with a tumultuous splash. Frigid water circled his body. Sven tried to stay afloat, his arms flailing as he tried to grab on to something to anchor him. Strong arms reached for him; he clung to them, appreciative for Stefan's assistance. Once back on the dock, he sat in a freezing puddle, grateful that at least the sun was shining overhead. The others surrounded him, asking if he was okay. Hell no, he wasn't okay. He was in pain and about to turn into an icicle.

The sound of an outboard motor at the end of the dock caught his attention. Sven was positive the two men were the same two men who had joined Gianni at the coffee shop at the top of the Fløien Mountain back in Bergen. Was this part of Gianni's efforts to deflect attention from his team? But why had he been the one to be targeted? The men knew he and Gianni worked together. *Dammit!* As soon as he dried off and got back to his hotel room, he was going to check in with Gianni and find out what the hell was going on. Staging a small incident with Team One was one thing, but targeting him was another. It wasn't an accident. And his face hurt like hell. He could feel his left cheek swelling despite the cold wash it had just received.

"Are you all right?" Sondra asked while Stefan, again, extended his hand to help him stand.

"No! What do you think? I've just been knocked over, and my face hurts like hell. Let's get the hell out of here."

"I'm sure the men here can help you clean up a bit before we move on." Bob joined them, no worse for wear. "In the meantime, we should probably report this incident."

"They're long gone and out of sight." Sven brushed the icy water from his hair. "Let's just forget it and move on up to Honningsvåg while the weather holds. I can get changed at the hotel before we leave town."

"Good idea." Bob squinted his eyes at him. "But it looks like you're getting quite a shiner on your left cheek."

"He's right," Sondra confirmed. "Better get that checked out while we're in Hammerfest."

Sven reached up and swiped his fingers over his cheek. Blood coated his hand. It was sore to the touch. Gianni had better have a credible account as to why his men had targeted him.

Chapter Eleven

"I'm not at all surprised that Sven wants to cancel the rest of the research." Conner turned toward Lars as their leader maneuvered their SUV along the coastal highway the following morning. He shook his head, trying to figure out what was behind Sven wanting to shut down the project. The obvious reason, in his mind, was that he was the one heading up the ring's operation. Both teams still had several larger operations along the North Cape that were on their list to inspect. If he had his way, they'd bypass these stops, make their way directly to Honningsvåg, and arrive before the other team.

"If he's involved in any of the rumors of a black-market operation, then I have to agree with you," Lars confirmed. "But so far, he seems to be on par with his team and his research. There are no signs he's the one responsible for any of the mishaps we've experienced. I'm sure Bob would have made anything unusual known at the meeting yesterday."

"But Sven's part of the federation, like you say." Brianna sat forward from the back seat to join in the conversation. "Wouldn't they be aware of his activities?"

"Not necessarily." Lars chuckled. "A good way to sweep his covert operations under the rug. And make it look as if someone else is responsible."

"But how can we prove it?" Brianna asked.

"Good question," Conner agreed. "Bob's on it, I'm

sure. I'm surprised he isn't the one being targeted instead of us, if for no other reason than to shut him up. The guy has been snipping at everyone every chance he gets."

"He certainly is caustic enough to rub anyone the wrong way." Lars slowed the SUV down to navigate a sharp curve along a mountainous pass before he continued up the side of the steep mountain road. "Do you really think Bob is involved in the operation? That he's trying to deflect his involvement onto someone else?"

Brianna sat back as the SUV continued up the steep incline. Memories of their mishap along the Geirangerfjord still lingered. Thankfully, the drop-off was on the driver's side of the road, across from where she was sitting in the back seat. Still, she hunched back in her seat, her thoughts focusing on the current conversation. The thought of Bob being involved never crossed her mind. Yes, he seemed determined in his quest to prove Sven's involvement. Yes, Bob could be caustic, but the way he'd been targeting Sven from the get-go didn't equate to him being part of their operation. And she was sure Helen would have had Bob vetted before she asked him to be part of the project. First chance she got, she was going to have another talk with Bob when they reached Honningsvåg. Perhaps she should contact Helen first. Let her know what was going on.

Although the scenery up along the coast had been captivating, their various stops along the way didn't reveal anything out of the ordinary. They were short and disappointing as far as their research was concerned. Although the fish count was low in this region and there was minor evidence of a virus and effects of climate warming, there were no reports of strange or unusual boats or people in the areas. The fishing operation managers were happy to comply with their research and questioning. Nothing seemed amiss.

From the mainland, they drove through the North Cape Tunnel, a 696-foot, below-sea-level, four-mile tunnel that took them to Magerøya Island plateau and Honningsvåg. Although the weather was pleasant enough, a cool breeze along the coast had kicked up. By the time they arrived in Honningsvåg, Brianna was definitely in need of a heavier jacket. Checking into their hotel next to the harbor took minutes. Conner accompanied her to their suites on the second floor.

"As I indicated, our rooms are connected." Conner took her key card and inserted it for her. "If you need anything while we're here in the next couple of days, don't hesitate to knock on the door." He handed her the oblong key card, stepped toward his own room, and paused. He turned to her as if to make sure she was okay.

"Thanks, Conner, but I'm sure there is ample security here. I'll be fine."

"Nevertheless, I'm here if you need me."

"First thing I need is something hot to warm my insides."

"I suspect there is a coffee pot in the room. I overheard the receptionist tell Lars that there are complimentary baskets of scones of some sort in each room. Gotta love room service."

"A hot cup of tea, a couple of scones, and a chance to get warm sounds good right about now."

"I'd join you, but I have to make a phone call. I received a text about my next assignment, and I need to follow up on it ASAP."

"Oh, do you know where you've been assigned?"

"Not yet. But I'm about to find out. I hope it's somewhere a bit warmer."

His laugh had her joining in as they stood in the hallway next to their hotel suites.

"Something tropical right about now would be nice," she agreed.

"We'll catch up with everyone in the morning. I hear the other team has already arrived. They've made good time as well. It should be interesting to see how their research is going."

As soon as Conner closed the door behind her, Brianna dropped her small carry-on luggage, turned on the hot pot, reached for her cell phone, and called Helen. It should be early enough in France, time-wise, for Helen to still be awake. Surprisingly, her boss picked up on the second ring.

"Brianna. How's it going?" Helen's no-nonsense tone sounded clear over the lines.

"I hope you have a minute to talk. I have some serious issues to discuss." Brianna sat on the mid-sized, overstuffed chair in the corner of the room next to the window that overlooked the harbor. She was becoming accustomed to all the Norwegian harbor views. Although the harbor was busy, she had a sense of relaxation as she watched the activity. The evening twilight still high and shining down on the water shimmied in the wake of the soft waves.

"Oh, dear. You sound concerned. I hope you're all right."

"I know I should have reported this earlier. At first it didn't seem to be much of a concern. However, things are progressing, and I'm starting to get more nervous."

"I did hear about Ivan, if that's what you're talking about."

"That and the fact that Conner and I were in a couple of mishaps prior to my uncle's boating incident."

"Oh, my goodness. I didn't hear about that. What happened? Are you okay?"

"Yes, we're okay," she assured her boss before quickly relating the events leading up to their last meeting with Mr. Erickson and Sven suggesting they shut the project down.

"My main reason for calling is to ask you about Bob Wilkins. He's been finger-pointing Sven Olson as being involved, if not leading a black-market ring here in Norway, and thus, the reason for the low catch reporting all along the coast. But it's been indicated that perhaps Bob might be the one leading the pack."

"What? You're kidding? Right?"

Brianna understood Helen's shocked surprise at such a thought. She'd had similar feelings herself. But Bob's actions suddenly appeared to be suspect.

"I don't know who came up with that scenario, Brianna, or the idea that Bob would even be involved in anything so underhanded. I can tell you he's only ever been up-front and aboveboard in all our dealings. He's never done anything that would lead me to doubt him and his credibility."

"That may be, but he's been over the top, fingering Sven to the point others are thinking he's using Sven to cover up for himself."

"Bob and I go back a long way. I can vouch for him. You need to follow his lead and concentrate on the mission at hand. If he thinks Sven is involved, you need to let your team leader, Lars, know so he can report it to the federation. Let the authorities deal with the possible black-market issue. As for Sven, there was no evidence of his involvement in Lobster Cove, so I can't say one way or the other if he is guilty. Again, let the authorities deal with that. Just stay on point with the mission at hand. And stay vigilant."

Where had she heard that before?

****

"What the hell were you thinking? Dammit, Gianni, I ended up with a black-and-blue eye and a swollen, bloodied cheek. I thought I said no major injuries." Sven stared at his reflection in the mirror over the sink. He looked as if he'd gone a couple of rounds in the ring with a heavyweight. Good thing he hadn't lost an eye or any teeth in the ordeal.

"I have no control once my men are on the job. You should be happy they hurt you and not someone else. Takes you off the guilty list."

"That may be, but I don't appreciate what I look like and how I feel. Are you trying to take me out, Gianni? Are you attempting to take over and walk away with everything? Because if you are, I can assure you your days will be numbered. You won't get away with it."

"No! No! What gave you that idea? Of course I'm not. We are working together."

"Don't cross me, Gianni. I haven't come this far without incident just to have you mess it up for me. Be careful, my friend. Do not cross me!"

"Do not cross me!" Gianni grated back at him over the phone. "I will meet you at the North Cape, as planned."

Before Sven could reply, Gianni ended the call. *Dammit!* He didn't trust the man or his cronies at this point. If he ever laid eyes on those two thugs again, they'd be sorry. He couldn't wait for this operation to be over. And that went for the federation's mission as well. He needed to keep his status with the committee and the federation on a positive note.

And make sure his contacts down the line remained satisfied.

****

Brianna met Conner and Lars for breakfast in the hotel's spacious dining room the following morning. It was a great peaceful start to a clear and sunny day in Honningsvåg. The sun streamed through the large windows behind the breakfast bar. She was eager to drive up to the northern end of the plateau and finally stand next to the North Cape monument. The drive should be scenic and relaxing. She spotted Bob, Sondra, and Stefan seated at a circular table several tables over. She waved a morning greeting, only to be brought up short as they stiffly nodded, then quickly put their heads together as if to shut her out. Suddenly not so sure what the day would bring, she turned back to Conner and Lars to see if they had witnessed the other team's reaction. But the two men also had their heads together, talking in low tones so she couldn't make out what they were discussing.

What the hell was going on?

Sven suddenly rushed into the dining hall and came to an abrupt halt in front of their table. The three of them stared up at him.

"You aren't the only ones who have been involved in an accident," Sven announced and made a big production of removing his sunglasses as he leaned forward. "You see this?" he demanded, pointing to his swollen face. "A damn rowdy bunch of drunken men stumbled out of a harbor bar in Hammerfest yesterday afternoon and careened into us on the dock, knocked my face against a post, which had me tumbling into the frigid water. I almost drowned."

"Was anyone else hurt?" Lars asked, then turned to the table where the other members of Team One were staring at Sven as well. Lars' lack of concern for Sven was obvious. After all, the guy was still standing there—alive.

"No. Just me," Sven huffed, obviously affronted at Lars' lack of concern. "Like I said back in Tromsø, I think this project has gone on long enough. Before we're all banged up or dead."

Brianna was beginning to agree. How many more team members needed to be injured or killed? Ivan was still in the hospital, hanging on by a thread. She was feeling much better after her mishaps, but she was ready to call it quits before their final stop near the Russian border as well.

"I'll call Mr. Erickson before we head out to the cape." Lars stood and glanced over at Sondra. "In the meantime, I suggest we take the day off and relax and treat this as a personal day. Take advantage of an excursion not connected with the project. Unwind."

Brianna couldn't agree more. In fact, it's what she had psyched herself up for when she woke up this morning. Both teams needed the break. Although she'd not had major repercussions from her own incidents, Sven's encounter was a reminder that no one was safe. As Helen had advised—stay vigilant.

Conner pushed his chair back, circled the table and put his hand around her shoulder, as if he'd read her thoughts. "Let's take a drive out to the cape. I understand there's a reindeer operation midway. We can stop in and check it out. Should be a relaxing drive."

"What about Lars?" She glanced over to where their leader was now standing next to Sondra, in deep discussion. Although being alone with Conner without the others was enticing, she wasn't sure it was a good idea. Her feelings for him had grown out of proportion. She knew he wasn't into a long-term relationship. Still, it would allow her to spend a relaxing day seeing the sights and finally reaching the North Cape.

"Lars has other plans this morning. He said he'd meet us all at the cape later this evening. It'll give us plenty of time to wander the area along the way and enjoy what the North Cape has to offer once we reach the top."

How could she refuse such a tempting offer? Not to mention his enticing and charming smile. And knowing he no longer suspected her uncle's operation was under suspicion. "I'd like that, thanks."

The drive took them through the magnificent subarctic landscape of Finnkirka, toward the most northern point of Norway along the E69 Highway. Herds of grazing reindeer and several Sami camps, indigenous to this part of the world, dotted the hillsides. The sight reminded her of many of the white-tailed deer herds prevalent in the hills of New York. With Wild and Wonderful's penchant to protect both flora and fauna, and especially the environment as a whole, Brianna never tired of observing the world around her when on assignment. And as much as she had been to Norway previously, this was the first time she'd had the opportunity to experience driving through reindeer country. She was going to have to get her parents to venture farther afield in Norway when they came to visit the family. Her father, especially, would enjoy the scenery.

Midway to the cape, they ran across a small reindeer outcropping that sported a small Sami souvenir shop in the middle of nowhere. A huge, typical colorful crowned Finnmark cap sat high atop the roof over the open door. Nearby a gentleman dressed in the typical Finnmark outfit of red and blue, with a replica of the hat like the one over the shop door, was in the process of feeding several reindeer. A handful of visitors were already gathered around to take part in the experience and stretched their hands out to pet the animals.

Conner parked the car, and together they joined in the feeding frenzy. Despite the large antlers, the reindeer were actually on leashes of sorts and restrained by their owner. Still, Brianna was hesitant to get too close. Conner circled his arm around her waist and ushered her closer to the animals so she could pet the reindeer. His caring touch warmed her and sent a comforting feeling clear to her toes to have him protect her, steady her, and give her the confidence she needed to approach and pet the huge animal without fear of being bitten or attacked by the antlers. It was obvious these reindeer were well taken care of, and the few that meandered around the facility were more pet-like and accustomed to humans. Without looking at Conner, not wanting him to see the warmth that was more than likely evident in her flushed cheeks, she stepped forward and proceeded to run her fingers over the reindeer's forehead while the herder nodded, encouraging her.

"That wasn't so bad, now, was it?" Conner reached out to pet the reindeer as well.

She couldn't help but return Conner's grin and was surprised to see the pleased expression in his eyes. Had he also felt the connection between them when he'd wrapped his arm around her?

"Thanks to you. These animals are rather huge. Especially their antlers. I appreciate the support and encouragement. I'm not usually that frightened in a controlled environment."

"We've been through a lot lately. Come on, want to wander the fields and see how close we can come to those reindeer wandering about?"

She turned toward the opposite side of the shop where Conner had indicated. A path led farther afield where several visitors were already heading toward a large herd of grazing reindeer alongside the hillside. It reminded her, once again, that the Sami were legendary reindeer herders who still lived a nomadic life.

"As much as I like an adventure and don't mind hiking, I'd rather continue to the North Cape. This has been lovely, but I've been looking forward to the North Cape statue for a long time. The closer I get to it, the more I can't wait to be able to stand next to it." Not that she hadn't hiked New York's Finger Lakes trails a time or two. But being close to reaching her destination, she was eager to get there.

"Then let's check out the shop and see if they have something to snack on before we go."

A young boy, dressed in the traditional Sami outfit, greeted them with a warm, engaging smile as soon as they entered the shop. He enthusiastically started giving them his tour-guide speech.

"We are one of the ten percent of Sami that still keep reindeer for a living. During the winter months, the reindeer live off of moss they find under the snow on the mountain plains. In the summer, they graze along the coastal areas, in places like here, where we camp to tend to our herd. I hope you get a chance to pet them while you are here."

Conner assured the boy that they had already visited the reindeer and that they were interested in checking out their snacks.

"You will find dried reindeer meat, crowberry juice, and a variety of herbal teas. Enjoy."

Twenty minutes later, after enjoying their light snack, they were back on the highway headed toward the North Cape. Conner concentrated on driving while Brianna took in the scenery. The day had turned cloudless and sunny, and except for the breeze blowing off the ocean, Brianna couldn't have asked for a more perfect day to explore the cape. With Conner.

Chapter Twelve

Brianna couldn't believe she'd finally reached the North Cape where the famous Arctic marker stood on the northern tip of the island. And they had reached it without incident. The breathtaking view atop the 1,000-foot-high cliff, with a slight breeze cooling the hot afternoon sun, was nothing short of exhilarating. And they hadn't even approached the magnificent globe monument yet.

After parking the car, they approached a series of round stone disk sculptures edged in bronze. A large sign indicated the sculptures were started in 1988 and referred to as "Children of the World." A mother and child monument pointed toward the seven disks. As she and Conner walked between the sculptures, erected in a semi-circle, they took the time to read the symbolisms depicted on each.

"Now there's an interesting disk." Conner pointed to the one labeled "Rabble Rousing" and chuckled. "I bet it was a young boy who came up with that one."

"No doubt." Brianna laughed. "Remind you of someone you know? Somehow I can't picture you as a rowdy kid."

"All kids can be a bit rowdy. I bet you were, too."

"You're evading my question." She grinned up at him. "Not ready to admit you weren't the serious kid you seem to be today?"

"I might have been rowdy, but I wasn't a delinquent. I was always too busy helping out at home when I wasn't playing sports. Again, how about you?"

She looked over to another stone and pointed. "I was more of a 'Peace and Justice' child. I think that's why working for Wild and Wonderful appeals to me."

He took her hand and led her toward the North Cape Hall building on their left. The large white dome rose above the roofline. The large skeletal metal globe loomed farther out, closer to the ledge of the plateau.

"These disks are a great tribute to the children of the world, as it implies," Conner commented, then turned toward her, a serious expression on his face this time. "Speaking of children, why aren't you married with children by now?"

Her hand tightened in his. She was shocked by his change of topics. Especially as it was a more personal question. One she hadn't anticipated. It gave her pause. It wasn't as if she'd never thought about having children someday. But finding the right father for her children hadn't happened yet. She thought she had found that special someone with Carl, but obviously, he hadn't felt that she was very special. Not sure how to respond, she decided to keep it simple.

"The situation hasn't presented itself yet, I guess. What about you? I don't see a ring on that finger." Even though he had indicated earlier that there was no one, she couldn't help turning the tables on him and asking for clarification.

"Touché. We seem to be in the same boat. Maybe neither of us have met the right person." He tugged on her hand again, pulling her forward. "Come on. That gigantic globe is calling to us."

Glad for a change in subject, Brianna kept pace with his strides, and within minutes they were standing right where she had longed to be—next to the famous black metal globe monument marking the northernmost point in Europe, the North Cape. And with Conner Holt standing next to her. Her heart beat triple time. She could now cross this experience off her bucket list.

Conner, however, didn't seem enthralled with the globe itself. He was watching her instead. His dimpled smile played havoc with her thoughts. And her equilibrium.

"I suspect you've been here before," she stated, eyes now glued to the globe. "With all your research and travels in the northern hemisphere, I can't believe you'd miss this one."

"Actually, I have been here. I can even give you the five-cent tour of the hall, if you like."

"Lead the way, and don't leave anything out." She was pretty sure Conner could see the excitement written all over her face, not able to hide her delight.

"We should get a picture first." He stopped her, pulled out his cell phone, positioned her next to the globe, stepped back, and snapped a couple of shots before she could respond.

He was right. She wanted the memory.

"Thank you. What about you?" she asked. "Or do you already have pictures of all the sites you've visited?"

"A few. But this one would be special. Why don't we get one of the both of us together?"

Again, he didn't give her a chance to reply. Instead, he positioned himself next to her and placed one arm around her shoulders in a snug grip while he extended the other, cell phone in hand. She couldn't help but smile up at him only to see the flash of his cell phone go off. Then, without warning, he swung her against his solid chest, leaned over, and kissed her full on the lips. She heard another snap of the cell phone.

OMG! How was she even going to respond to his kiss? A full-blown, deep, prolonged kiss making her want to wrap her arms around him, pull him in even closer, and kiss the living daylights out of him in return?

"I'll download these to your phone so you can have a couple as well." He stepped aside and returned his phone to his pocket as if nothing had happened between them. "Come on, there is a lot to check out inside the hall." He took her hand and led her to the building.

Brianna could only follow. Her mind a whirl with what had just taken place. He had to have felt something, too. A connection between them. So why was he suddenly acting as if it didn't mean a thing?

"The North Cape Hall, unbelievably, is open all year round," Conner narrated as they walked up the steps toward the entrance, suddenly becoming a tour guide. "The stone structure was started in the 1950s, but the building complex took place in the 1980s. It was erected in 1988 and became a popular tourist attraction."

He led her through the hall's various centers, including a small museum and a video cinema with a wide-screen system showing a film about the four seasons on the cape and a chance to witness the amazing display of the midnight sun. Exhibitions depicted the underground tunnel and the history of the North Cape as a destination for travelers. Her mind was still on Conner. And that kiss.

On their way out of the building, Brianna spotted the gift shop.

"Let's go in and see what they have." She hadn't thought about collecting souvenirs, being too focused on their assignment, but she suddenly felt the need to have a reminder of her time exploring the coastal waters—with Conner. She circled the shop until she came to a selection of various jewelry that displayed a myriad of colorful stones. She immediately fell in love with a deep-pink, heart-shaped necklace. The shopkeeper quickly came to her side to see if he could assist her, a broad smile on his face. He lifted the necklace from the display case and handed it over the counter for her inspection. She wrapped her fingers around the stone and rubbed its smooth surface with her thumb. The stone felt warm in her hand. She immediately knew she had to have it.

"The stone is a thulite palm stone," the shopkeeper informed her. "It's known to clear and activate both the heart chakra as well as the eye chakra, which helps the wearer to view the world with much love."

Love. Romance. She thought about how her feelings for Conner had grown over the last two weeks, and his more recent kiss. She was rational enough to realize that although nothing could come of their relationship, she would at least have a memento of their adventures together.

"We'll take it." Conner stepped up beside her. He pulled his wallet out and handed the salesclerk a handful of bills before she had a chance to do so herself.

"Really, Conner. I can pay for it myself."

"Nonsense. A gift from me to you. It'll be a reminder of all we've gone through together the past couple of weeks—both bad and good. And as an apology for my doubting your family's connection. Overall, it's been lovely sharing this adventure with you."

Lovely? A token of love? From him? If only.

"Thank you. It's kind and thoughtful. And I don't blame you for not trusting my family. I was concerned as well."

"I understand."

"Again. Thank you for this. I'll treasure it as a token of all we've shared on this journey, too."

He smiled down at her. "Hopefully, a connection that will survive long after this project is completed."

Speechless, she finally found her tongue, but before she could respond, he took the necklace from her trembling fingers and placed it around her neck. The shopkeeper stood by, watching, a wide grin on his face. He obviously thought they were a couple. Good Lord, she felt her face flush, just wishing they were a couple. And that their connection would last for a long time to come.

She grasped the stone in her hand, looked up at Conner, and blinked at the way he was gazing into her eyes. He stepped closer, lowered his head as if he were about to kiss her, but then placed his hands on her shoulders and leaned back.

"It looks good on you." His caring expression had her heart thumping.

Had he wanted to kiss her again? As much as she wished he had?

"Thank you." She emitted a trembly whisper. She would treasure it always.

As they exited the hall, Conner led her to the left where there was a fence line at the northern edge of the steep rocky cliff overlooking the calm waters of the Barents Sea far below. Nothing short of amazement washed over her as she stood at the edge of the flat outcropping and gazed out to sea. Sharp, jutting cliffs rose in the distance. She wrapped her lightweight jacket a little tighter as she looked out over the edge of the island and down below into the vast, deep, ice-blue ocean that sparkled far out into the distance. The ocean's mist rose, and only fresh scents of mist permeated the air around them, filling Brianna's senses with a freshness she was coming to relate with Norway and especially the Arctic. And Conner.

Walking the perimeter, they took in the vastness of the ocean. A few ships, including a cruise ship, sailed the calm waters down below. They looked like small rubber toys bouncing around in a bathtub. Conner nudged her arm and pointed toward the left of the plateau where a truck was parked next to an assortment of vehicles close to an embankment without guardrails. Not the parking area where they had parked their car earlier, but one that seemed to be unattended and open in cases of overflow. Brianna was surprised that there was no fencing in the area despite the deep drop-off and stony crevice outcropping.

"Does that truck look familiar to you?" he asked, never taking his eyes off the truck.

She hadn't noticed the truck, too busy enjoying the scenery in front of her. Now she tried to focus on the vehicle he had indicated. "Not really, no. Should it?" She wasn't sure where he was going with this, especially way out here at "land's end," her mind focused on being on top of the world. With Conner by her side.

"Look closer. What do you see?"

They walked toward the vehicles, trying to get closer in order to get a better look. She wasn't sure what he was talking about, but she couldn't help but notice the two men who seemed to be arguing, which suddenly led to a pushing and shoving match.

"Oh, my God! Isn't that the men who were talking to Sven at the hospital?" She gasped and stopped, clutching Conner's arm.

"Good catch." He put his hand in front of her as if to protect her. "We should find Lars. He should be here by now."

But before they could turn to go look for their leader, Sven stepped out from around one of the parked vehicles and approached the two men. The men turned on Sven and started punching him. Sven fell to the ground, tried to get up, but was knocked back down with a blow to his head. The two men continued to argue, then started punching each other with more force this time. In awe, Brianna wrapped her arm around Conner and clung for dear life. He enfolded her in his arms, pulled her close, and stopped.

An anguished piercing scream rent the air as not one but both men toppled over the side of the cliff into the deep gorge, out of sight. Sven scrambled to his feet and rushed to where the men had toppled over the ledge. He peered over the edge, his hands on his knees for support. Behind him, another man came to Sven's side.

"What the hell just happened?" Conner asked.

She was shaking too much to utter a single word, even if she knew the answer. There was no way either of those two men could have survived such a fall—the ragged mountainside would surely see to that.

"And who is that guy standing next to Sven? I recognize him but can't place him."

Brianna tried to pull herself together. "I don't recognize him, but he seems to know Sven."

They watched as Sven finally stood and turned to the gentleman standing next to him. Apparently, they were now having words with each other. Sven swiftly moved from the edge of the ravine and did a fast walk back to the area where several vehicles were pulling in, slamming on the brakes. Brianna could hear the gears grinding as they came to a halt. Several officers jumped from their cars and rushed toward Sven.

"What the hell is going on now?" Conner cursed.

In shock, she watched as the officers quickly handcuffed Sven. Two other officers chased after the man that had been talking to Sven, who had suddenly taken off running in the opposite direction.

A crowd suddenly materialized, including Sondra, Bob, and Stefan. Brianna kept pace with Conner as he started to rush toward the other team members.

"Look." Brianna gasped. "There's Lars. Where did he come from?"

"Not sure, but we're going to find out."

"Why am I the one in handcuffs? I was standing here minding my own business when those two thugs attacked me." Sven was shouting at the security guard when they arrived on the scene. "I tried to break up their fight and asked them what was wrong. See if I could help. That's when they started in on me. Next thing I knew, one shoved the other, and they started fighting. Before I knew it, they were catapulting over the edge. I have nothing to do with them."

"Do you have any idea who they are?" the policeman asked Sven as a rescue crew arrived, lights flashing. Several paramedics gathered their equipment and headed to the ledge.

"No. I'm here with my team from the federation.

Those thugs came out of nowhere and started fighting between themselves. I tried to stop them before they ended up over the edge. Apparently, I was too late."

"What about the man who you were just talking to?" the policeman questioned.

"No. Never saw him before, either."

Brianna knew Sven was a liar. The two men who went over the cliff, screaming and waving their arms in the air, were the same men she and Conner had seen Sven talking to back at the hospital. She didn't recognize the Italian-looking gentleman who had taken off running across the plateau. Listening in to the officer's interrogation of Sven, she could only ascertain that Sven was involved in some way. And the officials had to know about his involvement if they had handcuffed him. And it could only be that he was part of the black-market operation that was walking off with the fish from the Nordic coastal waters and selling them for a profit.

All eyes turned to several security men who rushed past them, giving chase to the man who had been talking to Sven before he took off running.

"Don't worry," the officer holding Sven said. "We have the area surrounded. He won't get far."

"What the hell is going on?" Sven shook his hands behind his back. "Get these off me!"

"The federation alerted us. They received notice that you are the one in command of a black-market operation funneling fish through Norway to Italy, then on to Asia."

Brianna wrapped her arm around Conner's and clung. She sighed and shook her head as Bob stood, watching, a wide grin on his face. His suspicions were confirmed. He stood tall, then stuck out his arm and pointed toward the man running along the cliff. "I'm sure that's his accomplice."

"Oh, my God! That guy is going to jump," Sondra screamed.

Stefan came to her side to support her. Sondra hid her face in his shoulder.

Brianna turned just in time to see the man vault over the fence and plunge into midair and the ocean far below.

"He will not get far," the official said. "We have many coast guard at the ready. If he survives the plunge."

"I have heard from Mr. Erickson." Lars stepped forward as the officers led Sven away. "As long as we are all here—what's left of us—he will meet us back at the hotel in Honningsvåg this evening to wrap things up."

Brianna was all for wrapping things up. Hand in hand, she walked alongside Conner to their car on the other side of the hall. Hopefully, this would put an end to the rumors that her uncle's operation was involved in any wrongdoing.

On the other hand, she wasn't happy to be parting ways with Conner, once she left Norway and headed back home. She had finally found someone she would love to spend the rest of her life with. He was caring, honest, protective, and a great kisser. She had enjoyed sharing her adventures with him. Just being in his company had her wanting to spend more time with him. But she knew he wasn't the settling-down kind of guy.

Chapter Thirteen

The drive back to Honningsvåg was uneventful. Conner concentrated on driving while Brianna napped in the front seat next to him. Glad she had overcome her injuries from their initial accident, he was still concerned for her well-being. He wasn't sure how all this was going to end, but one thing was for certain. How in the hell was he going to be able to walk away and leave Brie behind? That kiss at the North Cape had upended him in more ways than one. What was he thinking? Kissing her like that? It didn't matter that he'd been taken in by her from the start. Yes, he more than enjoyed her company. She was smart, caring, enthusiastic, dedicated, and he had loved every bit of their time together. Well, except for the accidents. Those he wished had never happened. But it had drawn him closer to her. But that kiss. She had to have felt the sparks between them.

And whatever had possessed him to pay for that beautiful heart-shaped stone necklace? Seeing it on her only increased his desire to pull her into his arms and kiss her again. But to what end? *Damn*. It had been hard to hold back. He was kicking himself now as he rounded another corner along the slopes of the highway leading back to Honningsvåg. He looked over at her now and wondered if she would consider sharing another adventure with him. Their time together was coming to an end. He didn't want it to end.

They had one more day in Honningsvåg. Regardless of how the meeting with Mr. Erickson went tonight, he planned on checking out their last fishery operation to complete his report on climate change before heading to his next assignment. He'd love nothing more than to have her join him. But would she? After all they'd been through. He wasn't so sure she'd be willing to give him a chance to prove to her...what? That he had fallen for her?

He slowed the SUV, turned to her, and felt his heart accelerate. Had he finally found that perfect someone?

****

Maxwell Erickson, director of the Norwegian Fishing Federation's current Arctic Project, sat at the head of the long, oval table. A somber silence filled the room. Everyone eyed each other as if waiting for the proverbial other shoe to drop.

"Well, I can't say that this is the way I had intended to conduct our final meeting, but it seems the federation has decided to bring this project to a close, after all. If you will bear with me, I will give you the rundown of the past two weeks' events, as we now know what has transpired. Please save any questions until the end."

Bob Wilkins, Lars Jensen, and Sondra Sølreida all leaned forward in concentration, their elbows up against the table. Brianna, along with Conner and Stefan Dutlov, sat back, hands folded in their laps, waiting for Mr. Erickson to continue.

"According to an informant from Maine, Sven Olson was identified as the leader of the black-market ring with connections to Norway, specifically. Thus, his arrest earlier today. He fled to Norway and joined his family's fishing operation and the Norwegian Fishing

Federation. His family's fishery was never under suspicion and has been relieved of any wrongdoing. As well as several other suspected operations that have been cleared."

Once again, Brianna could see the satisfied look on Bob's face. She didn't blame him. She wondered if that tip had funneled through him, and thus the reason he was put on the same team as Sven in order to help keep an eye on his activities and contacts.

"Once it was reported to the federation, they had hoped to draw Mr. Olson out by assigning him to the project. The federation became more suspicious when he suggested shutting down the program at our last meeting, due to all the mishaps that had been happening. The federation's suspicions became more intense. Now here is where it becomes more evident of the scope of the black-market group's attempt to stop the project."

Mr. Erickson went on to explain that Sven's main contact, a Gianni Santino, was the one who had jumped off the North Cape cliffs, was captured, and confessed that he'd been working with Sven as his main contact in the operation. The two men who fell into the ravine, who were also working with Mr. Santino, were airlifted to the hospital. They later died from multiple wounds. Ivan Alexander, on the other hand, had been released from the hospital and returned home to his family to recuperate.

"The operation has come to an end," Mr. Erickson finally stated. "We do, of course, request your final reports and statistics before you leave Norway. The federation will take it all under advisement and proceed as we see fit. We thank you for your service, and we apologize for all the problems you have faced while engaged in this project."

Brianna and Conner had gone through a lot together. Luckier than the others, including Sven's cohorts, she had weathered her injuries and walked away from death's door. In truth, she was glad the project was shut down. She'd kept up with her reports daily. They were ready to be submitted to the federation. So where did she go from here? With Wild and Wonderful?

With Conner?

After a quick call to Helen Mapes to update her boss in regard to the project being discontinued, Brianna was given the go-ahead to take the rest of the time to simply enjoy herself before returning to New York.

"Why not take the ship back down to Bergen, relax, and enjoy each of the ports of call along the way?" Helen suggested. "It's great that your uncle's operation was given a clean slate. I'm sure that's taken a heavy load off your mind."

"Yes. In fact, as long as I don't have to be back right away, I might stop in Tromsø to visit them and make sure everything is up and running properly after that boating incident."

"Glad they caught up with the lead culprit that was causing so much trouble."

So was Brianna, as was the rest of the federation and team members.

"Just so you know, I don't have any other projects needing your expertise at the moment. Still working on this problem here in France. I'll be in touch in a week or so."

As much as she liked an adventure and enjoyed doing marine biology research, Brianna was glad to be given a pass on a new project.

Sailing down the Nordic Coast was just the ticket

she needed to recoup. Who could resist leisurely time in the land of the midnight sun? After a soothing shower and snuggled in her pink flannel jammies, Brianna turned down the covers, preparing to call it a night, when there was a knock on the connecting door. Conner, as usual, was in the room on the other side of the knock.

"Brie, are you still up? We need to talk." He jiggled the door handle.

Not sure what they still had left to say to each other, after their brief exchange in regard to the program after the meeting, she turned the lock and swung the door open. And immediately found herself wrapped in Connor's arms, his lips covering hers. Taken aback momentarily, she gave in to his embrace. If this was his way of talking, she was ready and willing to do more than chat.

Without breaking his hold, he ended the kiss, only to look deep into her eyes. His were full of desire, questioning.

"I think I finally found someone I want to spend the rest of my life with, Brie. What about you? You've got to feel the same way I do whenever we're together. We make a great team."

Speechless, overwhelmed, she lifted up onto her tiptoes and kissed him with a passion she hoped answered his question. She then snuggled into his chest, her head resting on his shoulder.

"I was so afraid I'd never see you again once we left Norway," she whispered.

"Fat chance. I'm serious about working as a team. I have my new assignment. Feel like joining me someplace tropical?"

"I thought you'd never ask. Where are we going?"

"Right now, your bed is calling to us. We'll work out all the details tomorrow."

After all they'd been through, she was more than happy she was about to make a warmer Arctic connection. With Connor.

Epilogue

Brianna couldn't believe she was actually lying in a chaise lounge on a secluded beach in Tahiti, the evening sun dipping over the edge of the sparkling ocean. The fragrance of the various blooms filling the air. It was the most surreal feeling to actually be here, and to be hopeful that she wasn't dreaming. She'd missed Conner like crazy after he left for his next assignment. She had returned home to check on her parents and to prepare her final reports on the Arctic Project for Wild and Wonderful. She hadn't heard from him in weeks and had given up hope that she'd ever see him again. They had spent their last week in Norway together—day and night. So not to hear from him once they left Norway had dimmed her hopes of ever seeing him again.

Now she was in seventh heaven. He'd contacted her several weeks after he'd left, and had arranged a plane ticket for her to fly out to meet him in Tahiti, a tropical paradise. Of course, she couldn't refuse. He was done with his assignment, which had taken him farther into the outback than anticipated, and had been beyond communication. Of course she had jumped at the chance to reunite with him.

Having only arrived yesterday, she was now waiting for him to join her on the private beach cove outside the small cottage they were sharing.

"Sorry to keep you waiting, Brie." Conner handed

her a mai tai, sat on the edge of his chaise lounge, and raised his glass toward her.

She tapped the tip of her glass against his, and together they sipped their drinks.

"I want to apologize again for not contacting you sooner, Brie. It was impossible to get a connection from our remote location."

"I was worried something might have happened to you. Or that you'd forgotten all about me."

"No way I could ever forget you. In fact, I'm so glad you agreed to join me so we could resume our relationship. I've missed you so."

And she was more than ready to resume their relationship regardless of where it was headed. And right now, in this very romantic tropical location, she could only think about the present. And being this close to Conner again. Still, she wasn't blind to the fact that this could only be a simple moment in time.

"I'm here now, but I'm not sure how this will turn out once you go off on your next assignment." She sat on the edge of her seat, facing him. "Or me on mine. I'm sure our paths will never jive. And as you know that's not conducive to a long-term relationship."

"Exactly. That's why I want to make it a permanent one."

He stood, reached for her hand, and drew her up out of her seat. And into his arms. Right where she wanted to be.

"So what do you have in mind?" Dare she hope?

"For starters, I thought we'd make a great working team. We'd complement each other's work ethics and professional fields. It would be a win-win for both of us."

"You're talking a business deal?" she asked,

deflated. It's not what she'd been thinking. Hoping for.

"Not exactly." He reached into his pocket and withdrew an item that looked suspiciously like a ring. He then reached for her left hand and held a ring in his other hand. A ring that resembled the necklace he'd bought her at the North Cape. She looked at it and grew still. Then looked up into his pleading eyes.

"I thought we could make it a long-term, forever deal. I love you, Brie. I've loved you ever since that first day in Bergen."

"Oh, Conner. I love you too."

He pulled her into his arms and kissed her under the tropical palm trees and the glowing evening sun. She didn't hold back. She wrapped her arms around him and kissed him back, never wanting to let go.

"I take it that's a yes?" he asked, leaning his head against her forehead.

"If you're asking me what I think you are, then yes, that's a definite yes."

Her hand shook as he slipped the ring on her finger. She clasped the matching necklace that she'd worn since he'd placed it there. He kissed her ring finger, and her heart melted.

"I only have one request, Conner. I hope you agree." She couldn't help but smile as she clutched his hands in hers and met his questioning eyes.

"Do I dare ask?" He grinned.

"I'd like to have the wedding sooner, rather than later, and it would mean the world to me if we could have it take place at the North Cape."

"Your wish is my command. Done." He drew her against him, wrapped his arms around her, and kissed her—to seal the deal. And another Arctic connection.

A word about the author...

Carol Henry is a #1 best-selling author who writes award-winning, 5-STAR reviewed light romantic suspense adventures, as well as American historical, holiday, and contemporary light romance novels. A world traveler, Carol has written for several major cruise lines' deluxe in-cabin books and *Porthole Cruise Magazine*, but also takes great pleasure in weaving her own adventures with her "characters" in her Connection series novels. Even her contemporary novels, such as her Lobster Cove series, have a few snippets from her travels, as well. Visit her website: www.carolhenry.org.

Thank you for purchasing
this publication of The Wild Rose Press, Inc.

For questions or more information
contact us at
info@thewildrosepress.com.

The Wild Rose Press, Inc.
www.thewildrosepress.com